Kansas City Love Stories

Christopher Dye

Kansas City
Love Stories

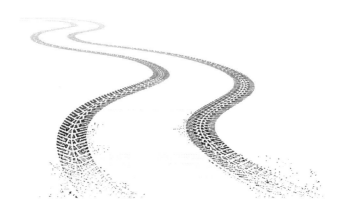

Christopher Dye

Kansas City Love Stories
© 2023 Christopher Dye

Cover and interior design: Lisa Carta
Illustration © Roberto Scandola | Dreamstime.com

ISBN 9798374109924

CONTENTS

I dedicate this book to my parents,
Stanley and Eleanor Dye—
he who urged me to write
and she who taught me how.

CHAPTER
1

It was exactly 5pm, when I walked out the door of the Trader's National Bank Tower in Kansas, City, Missouri, holding a cashier's check for $200,000 in one hand and the keys to a new Mercedes Benz 500 in the other. I raised my hands and howled at the top of my lungs because I had just pulled off an impossible coup! It had taken hours of negotiations and hard bargaining back and forth, but I had in my pocket the new partnership agreement under which I had made an almost unheard of lateral entry as a full partner into one of the top three law firms in Kansas City—Clauson, Schwarz, and Logue.

How, you ask, could a guy who was thirty-two years old, who had graduated fairly far from the top of his 125-member class at Cornell Law School, who got only one job offer after sending out storms of resumes—that being the response from Kansas City Legal Aid—make a lateral entry as a full partner into such an august law firm? Because, as it turns out, the real practice of law often has little to do with what is learned in law school and everything to do with how well you actually practice law. Though I had gotten low grades, I had also learned to advocate so well that my Cornell team placed second in the National Moot Court Trials in my last year of school. This, of course, lit up my resume. That and my faculty advisor's powerful recommendation had gotten me an invitation to join the Legal Aid Society of Kansas City, Missouri.

Many people look down on Legal Aid trial work, comparing it unfavorably to the work of trial lawyers in large, private firms, but the truth is—for all of you who want to be trial litigators—Legal Aid lawyering is a great beginning. It throws you into court almost immediately, where, in my case, I was mentored by Will Bunch, the best trial attorney I would ever encounter.

By the time of my lateral entry into Clauson, Schwarz, and Logue, I had tried more jury and court cases than any of my big firm colleagues, and I'd developed a knack for winning the trust of judges and jurors, the vast majority of whom take their jobs extremely seriously. Depending on the charge, if jurors convict a person, he or she could spend years in prison or, in the rare case, face execution. To succeed, a lawyer has to be completely forthright with the jurors. You cannot ever lie. Instead, you must focus unrelentingly on the prosecution's obligation to prove their case beyond a reasonable doubt. The court, of course, will carefully instruct the jury on this point. So your argument must focus on doubt, not clear facts. Somehow, I was very good at all of that, and word got around that I was a comer.

You will not be surprised to learn that law firms, like any other business, are operated to make money—lots and lots of money—most of it going to the partners. At the time of my interviews, there was a burst of a new class of criminal defendants, commonly called "white collar criminals." Any managing partner of a big law firm could see immediately the piles of cash to be made in the defense of these high earning felons who were desperate to stay out of the prison. The problem for the big firms was that they did not have attorneys who could try criminal cases, so people from these firms began to call me at Legal Aid, offering me jobs.

On the day in question, I had lined up interviews with three major firms: Kauffman & King; Clauson, Schwarz & Logue; and Cooke, Pardee & Hamm. I had terminated my interview with Kauffman & King because Julius King, the managing partner, had spent the whole interview standing up and looking down his long nose at me, telling me why he did not think that I was Kauffman & King material. (Julius never used his first name. He introduced himself as "J. Christian King," which is an indication of a truly ballooned ego.) I knew his first name, so throughout the entire interview, I called him "Julius." I could see that he did not like it.

Clauson, Schwarz & Logue was second on my list, and I showed up right on time at 9:00 am. Their managing partner, Martin Logue, had a reputation of being one of the toughest negotiators on the planet. I, however, was in the driver's seat because, as I had to remind him on several occasions during the eight hours it took us to get to agreement, that, for what he needed, I was the only game in town. To drive that home, I periodically glanced at my wristwatch and said, "Look, Marty, I've got to move this along because I've got a three o'clock at Cooke, Pardee & Hamm."

Marty was a lean man, impeccably dressed in a Saville

Row suit. I could see he was excruciatingly uncomfortable being in the weak position. He began squirming in his chair, and his color got redder and redder as his blood pressure rose. Finally, we hammered out a deal. We both realized that I would not agree to join the firm unless I was made a partner.

The lateral entry of a partner into a law firm was extremely rare and very difficult because it disturbed the established pecking order. A new entrant would take up a partner place that associates had hoped to occupy, and he would acquire partnership benefits that other partners had worked years to attain. My opening offer had been entry as a senior partner, which I knew Marty would *never* give me, but that gave me the negotiating tool of coming down to full partner. This would include the key benefit of a fully paid-up retirement package, which Marty would find hard to grant me.

Marty faced a dilemma: on the one hand, he and the other managing partners fully understood the gold mine of clients that I would draw to the firm, but on the other hand, a fully paid-up retirement package was something partners only achieved at retirement, after years of good work for the firm. Here, Marty and I argued back and forth much of the day. Finally, at about two o'clock, I looked at my wrist watch again, not subtly, and told him, "Marty, stop telling me that the managing partners won't agree. Why don't you go around to their offices and ask!"

Marty gave me one of the dirtiest looks I have ever seen, because he knew I was calling his bluff. Every partner in the firm, and probably some of the associates, fully understood that they needed me to cash in on the white-collar gold mine. So, in a false huff, he stood up and left his office, and in a truly childish expression of pique, it took him an hour and ten minutes to return—after the time scheduled for my appointment at Cooke, Pardee & Hamm. "OK," he snarled, "you've got it all, *except* for the fully paid-up retirement plan." Snarling even more he added, "Everyone thought you were just too greedy! That would cost us $200,000 now. But against my *strenuous* opposition, the partners agreed to give you a before-tax signing bonus of $100,000." His face was bright red, getting redder as each second passed. Then, just to pull his chain, I said, "There is one more thing." His face turned scarlet. "I want a Mercedes 500 as my partnership car—a brand new Mercedes 500." He looked at me and said, "We do that for all our partners. Even a jerk like you." I have since forgiven him for that last crass remark, particularly since he handed me the keys to the car, with the partnership agreement. "Partners arrive at 7:00 am, so be here on Monday," he said.

As I was standing on the sidewalk, someone pulled up in my Mercedes. It was gorgeous—a beautiful, deep, bluish gray, obviously a custom color, with bright, red leather seating and every option one could imagine. The driver rolled down the passenger window and said, "Hop in, Attorney Pace. You've gotta learn what all these buttons and dials mean before you start cruising around in this thing." He gave me a thorough primer and told me to take the manual home to make sure I knew all there was to know. The man's name was Oscar Calhoun, a forty-five-year-old Black man, who, I later learned, had been with the firm for years and was its in-house private investigator. Even a slow guy like me figured out quick that he was a guy I'd always want on my side.

As Oscar drove, I came to appreciate the incredible quality of the car. It was absolutely smooth, completely silent, and went from zero to sixty in no time at all. Once we got to my home on Harley Street, we changed seats, and Oscar helped me with the finer points of the machine. When I finally pulled into my driveway, he got out of the car, and I asked, "Mr. Calhoun, how are you going to get home?" And right on key, another firm vehicle, driven by Arleen Calhoun, pulled up to the curb. She was Oscar's wife, but also, as it turned out, she was to be my secretary, paralegal, and guardian angel throughout my career.

Mr. Calhoun walked me over to the car and introduced me, and Arleen and I took to each other immediately. Her approval validated the firm's decision to hire me as an advocate—she knew it was right from the start.

After they left, I went inside and upstairs to shower, then dressed and got into my beautiful Mercedes. I backed out of the driveway, drove around the block a couple of times, and headed down to the Plaza for Friday night drinks with the big crowd at Casey's Wild Irish Pub. But first, of course, I went to my bank and deposited my check.

CHAPTER
2

I swaggered into Casey's Wild Irish Pub feeling like I was king of the world. As I was working my way through the dense crowd at the long bar, Casey saw me, gave me a wave, and turned for the slow process of drawing my first Guinness from the tap. As I got within arm's reach, I noticed Dell Bondi sitting at the bar, a woman with a broad behind encased in very tight, new blue jeans. She was sipping from a glass of Johnny Walker Blue, with a full glass of the same next to her and ready to go. I recognized her immediately as one of the hottest real estate agents and developers in town. The rumor going around was that earlier in the week, she had closed on one of the biggest deals Kansas City had seen in years—the one hundred million dollar construction of a huge shopping center in the eastern part of Jackson County. This included a hotel, golf course, and casino nearby. Dell apparently netted a commission of $6 million for her firm, which included $2 million for her.

Once I reached the bar and got my Guinness, I worked my way down to where Dell was sitting and greeted her.

She recognized me, returned my greeting, put out her hand, and we shook. "Dell, congratulations," I said. "I hear you made a bundle and that all drinks tonight are on the house, thanks to you."

She looked at me briefly and replied with obvious disdain. "Are you nuts, Larry? You know I never give anybody anything for nothing."

I tried again. "Dell, those new blue jeans are really sharp. You look great!" She turned toward me with a half smile, her long, glistening, black hair framing her oval face and her stunning, gray-green eyes. With only a slight slur, she replied, "Yeah. I love these jeans too. But they're too damned tight and real hard to get off. After they're broken in, they're just great!"

"You know Dell, in your own way, you are one of the sexiest women around. So, maybe we can have dinner and then head to my place, where I would be happy to help you get those jeans off, pulled over your gorgeous rear end, and down your beautiful thighs to your ankles. Then you can help me get out of my pants and we can spend the night having fun together. How about it?"

She turned and looked at me briefly and sarcastically replied, "Well, ordinarily, I would never consider such an approach from someone I'd never dated and barely know, but since you're so suave, let's get going."

In one fluid movement, she ran her fingers through her shiny, black hair, pushing it back into a pony tail, which she fixed with a silver clip. She grabbed the bottle of Johnny Walker, jammed it into her large purse, gulped down the Scotch in one of the glasses, poured a finger into the other glass, stood up, and yanked me by the hand toward the door. We walked hand in hand toward her car. When we came to it, I stopped dead in amazement. It was an MG roadster that must have been at least ten years old, painted in that unique, rich, British Racing Green that MG was famous for.

At this point, we had our first fight. She wanted us to go to her house in her MG, and I wanted to drive both of us to my house in my gorgeous Mercedes. We back-and-forthed a little and then she said with a little more slur in her voice, "Get in my fucking car!"

So I did, and off we went, Dell in second gear, hitting sixty in no time. She sharply shifted up to three and four, taking each curve on the winding road to her house as much on the outside tires as she could. When the road crested onto the flat, she shifted up to fifth gear and floored it, roaring at eighty miles an hour for about a quarter of a mile until she slammed on the brakes with a huge screech and tire skid to come to rest in front of her home. She slowly turned into her driveway, cut the engine, and slurred, "Let's go."

We were barely through the door before we started grabbing and wrenching at each other's clothes. Eventually, I got her jeans down to her knees as promised and she had me in nothing but my boxer shorts. When she saw them, she hiccupped with some disdain, "So, I didn't figure you for that anti-sex underwear." But that and nothing else stopped us from making love until finally in the late afternoon on Saturday, we were both sexually exhausted. As I rolled off her, she rolled over onto her side and fell immediately into a deep-breathing sleep.

In the morning, I slid across the smooth sheets on her

king-size bed in her beautifully appointed bedroom. I was starving, because we hadn't had dinner. Looking for food, I found some Cheerios and milk in the kitchen and gulped them quickly before I started the coffee. As it brewed, I took a walk around her stunning home.

The magnificent kitchen was on the upper floor. It had top-of-the-line, custom appliances, real marble counter tops, and a huge, climate-controlled wine case. The dining table was situated across from the entry, centered on a huge picture window overlooking miles of the rolling hills of eastern Kansas. The view was so stunning that it literally took my breath away.

As well-appointed as the kitchen was, her food was of a different character. In the cupboards, I found rows and rows of canned vegetables, canned meat and fish, powdered milk, and coffee. I wondered what the refrigerator was for because it held only one bottle of milk and forty-eight bottles of beer, without a single fresh vegetable in sight.

For me, this would not do for a long weekend that would likely stretch through Monday night, so I immediately called Casey. In addition to his bar, Casey owned, with his son Joe, a little business called Casey's Gourmet Kitchen. Joe picked up the phone. I told him what I wanted and asked if he could deliver within a couple of hours. He paused, and said, "Larry, for you, we'll be there in a couple hours." He added, "We'll do our best, but we may be a little short on freshly made pasta." Their promise of quick delivery was related to the *pro bono* work I'd done for Joe three years ago, when I got his driver's license reinstated, notwithstanding the court's lifetime revocation of it. He'd been sober in AA ever since.

Joe showed up in only an hour and a half, just as Dell was coming upstairs for breakfast. He quickly brought five cardboard boxes of groceries into the kitchen. Dell watched in amazement as I pulled out three kinds of olive oil, caviar, arugula, portabella mushrooms, two filet mignon, pork tenderloins, heirloom tomatoes, goat cheese, prosciutto, fresh lox, a couple of baguettes that were still warm to the touch, my favorite three-cheese-prosciutto ravioli, and top-quality wines and whiskeys. The last box held several desserts, and as Dell watched me pull them out, I was afraid that the last course was the one she would start with.

When I was done unpacking the groceries, Dell looked at me puzzled, and said, "But none of this has been cooked."

"That's right, sweetheart. That's what I'm going to do."

"What?!" she exclaimed, as if she'd never heard of cooking.

I walked up to her, held her face in my hands, and kissed her softly. "Sweetheart, my dear, I am going to cook you real, healthy, gourmet meals, which will change your eating habits for the better, forever."

"I didn't know you could cook!"

"I'll do it. You help. Just please do as I ask," I said firmly.

In fact, I was pretty close to being a gourmet chef because I had learned to cook in law school at Cornell. One of the university's little known gems was its small dining room, located in Cornell's Statler School for Hotel Administration. Chefs-in-training prepared elegant meals there, all available for almost nothing. I can't remember how I found out about the dining room, but after my first dinner there, I met one of the students, a chef named Bernie Copperman. In exchange for some legal help, he let me go into the kitchen, where I watched the complex symphony of the creation of world-class, gourmet meals. Since then, I had tried to cook well whenever I could, and I brought all of my skills to bear on this Saturday night dinner for the marvelous lady I was falling in love with.

As we finished the last bite of dessert and sipped Bénédictine from crystal snifters, Dell looked up at me and said, "I don't know what to say, except that I'm falling fast for you." I could see from her eyes that she'd taken a risk. I took her two hands in mine and said, "I have never had an experience like this with anyone, and I will love you with all of my heart forever." We kissed, and then stood and hugged for a long time.

We headed for the bedroom again. Dell put on her nightgown and I climbed into bed, wearing just my shirt. We entwined our legs. I asked what movie she wanted to see.

"I've always loved *Pretty Woman!*"

So that is what we watched, holding hands. The only trouble was that we fell asleep about ten minutes after the movie started.

On Sunday morning, we slept late. When we finally dragged ourselves out of bed, I made, what I must say, was a magnificent brunch. As was the case the night before, she paid careful attention to how I cooked.

We spent Sunday afternoon walking along the beautiful Esplanade, window shopping and talking about things we wished we owned. Near the end of that stroll, she slipped her arm through mine, pulled tightly against me, and held me close.

We woke up Monday morning, sexually re-charged, so we were at it again until dinner time.

On Tuesday morning, we got up early because I needed to get to work by 7:00 am. She cooked my breakfast, trying to emulate the cooking style I had shown her, and it was a pretty damn good breakfast. We were out the door by 6:30. When we got back to my car, I stepped out of the MG and straightened up, as if I were a pocket knife whose blade had been extended fully. We met at the back of her car and kissed passionately for a few moments. Then, I backed away, and said, "Dell, I love you. Thanks for a great time."

"I don't know what to say," she said, "except that I have felt love for the first time in my life. Please be careful, and call me."

She hopped into the bright yellow, leather seat of her car and fired it up in a throaty roar, backed out, and quickly turned, heading toward Mason Street, shifting quickly up and down. As she made one of her trade-mark, high speed, ninety-degree turns left, she glanced in her rear view mirror, and waved her hand until she disappeared behind the Mason Building.

And that was the last I ever saw or heard from her for years.

CHAPTER
3

Flashes of my weekend with Dell, kept popping up like snapshots all day as I worked on contracts, appeals, and other documents. At about four o'clock, I took a break and dialed Dell's phone, but I only got an answering machine. Over the next two days, I called several times, but again and again I heard the same message.

On Friday, I called Dell's office and asked the receptionist to put me through to her. She paused for a couple of seconds and then said, "I'm sorry, but Ms. Bondi hasn't been with us for nearly a month."

I was stunned. I couldn't believe it. In a stern tone, I pressed her. "That cannot possibly be true. I just saw her this past weekend."

"I'm very sorry, sir, but that's all I can tell you. Why don't I put you through to Mr. Pasternak and he can talk with you."

I took a deep breath and slowly exhaled. Calming down, I replied, "Yes. I'd appreciate that very much."

Bill Pasternak picked up the phone immediately. "Sorry to bother you, Bill," I said, "but I urgently need to get in touch with Dell Bondi regarding a real estate matter that involved my firm several years ago."

Bill replied in a measured tone, "I can't tell you anymore than what Rebecca did. Dell withdrew from the partnership and took ou her share a month or so ago. We have heard nothing from her since. I have no idea where she is."

I thanked him and sank into my chair, stunned and unable to comprehend what he had said. Somehow, I managed to focus well enough on the urgent, deadline-sensitive work I had to complete that day. I finally finished my project late in afternoon and left the office earlier than I should have.

I drove up the winding road to Dell's home. As I rounded the last bend, I braked my Mercedes to a screeching stop. There, about a hundred feet up the road, was a large SUV parked in Dell's driveway. The sign on the side of the door read, "State Line Realtors: Your Straight Line to a New Home." I'd never heard of the firm!

I drove past the SUV and pulled to the curb across the street. A gray-haired, stout lady was pounding a sign into the ground. "Whose house is this?" I asked. She replied. "I have no idea."

"But, who authorized your putting this sign up?" I demanded.

"I believe it was some law firm."

"Which one?" I asked with burgeoning urgency.

"I'm not sure," she said. "My boss just told me to stick a sign up on the property. You're welcome to go in and take a look if you're interested."

I stared at her silently for a moment and then said, "Yeah. I'd like that."

Chapter 3

I opened the gleaming, glass door, with its long, custom, chrome handle and stepped inside. Apart from Dell's designer appliances in the kitchen, the house was completely empty, without a stick of furniture. Even the carpets had been removed, revealing gray, rough, concrete floors. I went down to the lower floor, and of course, it was empty, as well, although the view across the Missouri River and west toward Kansas was as gorgeous as it had been before.

I turned toward the door of the bedroom and paused for a moment before I entered. Here, for some reason, the shag carpet had been rolled up and pushed against one of the walls, but otherwise, the room was empty. I walked to the vast, walk-in closet and saw nothing but empty hangers. As I turned to leave, though, my eye caught a shadow of something in the back. I turned on the light and walked toward it. It seemed like some kind of cloth folded up on the floor, but as I picked it up and held it by the shoulders, I saw that it was the negligee Dell had worn for most of our weekend together. I knew immediately that I would never see her again. Even now, I can still feel the spike of anguish that stabbed me.

I reeled out of the closet, tight and rigid, as if trying to contain an explosion, but then, a pin was pulled and my grief and bereavement poured out of me in heavy, heaving sobs, tears pouring down my face. After each sob, I sucked in another lungful of air, sobbing again and again. "Why? Why?" I asked myself. How could she have just disappeared? She told me that she loved me. I thought we'd fallen in love.

I heard the real estate agent come into the house. She called down, "I've got to go now, but if you would like to stay,

I will leave the keys on the kitchen counter. I can pick them up in half an hour or so."

"No," I replied softly, "There is nothing for me here."

CHAPTER
4

I don't know how I got through the weekend, but somehow I managed to get to the office on time on Monday. I dove into my work. Gradually, over several months, the pleasure and excitement that I had always had for the law began to grind down my grief. Much to the amazement and deep satisfaction of Marty Logue, our senior partner, I was arriving at 6:30 in the morning and leaving as late as 10:30 at night, racking up billable hours by the dozens. Arleen's steady support and warmth helped me.

After a while, my life developed a rhythm of normalcy. I joined the Kansas City Racquet Club, and every Friday at five o'clock I headed to Casey's, where I drank my two bottles of Guinness and schmoozed and had dinner with friends.

During the work week, I spent my lunch hours at the library. My first time there, I saw a librarian standing near the end of the stacks carrying a load of books in her arms. She started walking toward me, wobbling oddly. I looked down and saw that she was wearing spike heels. She wobbled to the left, then to the right. One book slipped out of her grasp, then another, and all the rest followed in a thunder of thumps.

The last one hit the floor just as she reached the counter. She leaned on it and in two sharp, angry kicks, sent one shoe to the right and the other to left, mumbling under her breath, "I never want to wear these god-awful high heels again." She looked up at me and turned bright red. "I'm sorry," she said. "I should never have spoken that way."

"Well," I said, "it was tough for me. I've never heard a charming woman like you say 'god-awful' with such creative force!"

She looked up at me. For just a second, I thought she was going to punch me, but then she sheepishly said, "I'm a Methodist, so I've just committed a sin!"

"You really believe that?" I asked her.

"Not all the time. I'm cutting back," she said.

I looked down at her name tag: Virginia Wood, Chief Librarian.

"Ms. Wood," I said.

"Miss," she corrected me.

"I'm sure you do a wonderful job. It is tough to load and unload piles of heavy books, and we all appreciate it."

She gave me what, for Methodists, was probably a dark face, saying, "You're not trying to hit on me, are you?"

"I probably am," I said, "but in an absentminded way. I'm mainly here to see if you have some magazines I'm interested in—*Aviation Week & Space Technology*, *Forbes*, and *Foreign Policy*. Do you have them?"

"Only *Forbes*," she replied. "But we have a big budget, and I have substantial discretion in deciding what we buy, so I would be happy to look into getting the other two."

I glanced at my watch and said hurriedly, "Oh God, I'm

late. I've got to get back to the office." I spun around and sprinted out the door, across the street, and into our office building.

Back in our building, as I was riding the elevator up, I felt a tiny prick in my dormant libido. I said to myself, *She's tall, slim, and slouches a bit the way tall women do.* She had nothing like Dee's voluptuous body, which I was, even then, remembering in flashes. But there was something about her.

On Thursday, Arleen told me that the librarian had called and that Louis Nizer's *My Life in Court,* a book I had long ago requested, had arrived. I walked across the street to the library and went to the counter, where I told Miss Wood that I had come to pick up Nizer's book. I handed her my library card. She glanced at it and looked up. "You're Mr. Pace?"

"Yes, ma'am."

"I'm the chief librarian, Virginia Wood. I wish I could say that it is a pleasure to formally meet you, sir, however, this library card is over three years old. No one can borrow a book without a current library card. In addition," she said, after looking in her notebook, "I notice that you have incurred over $25 in *unpaid* library fines during the past three years."

She meant to be stern. There was a certain drill sergeant way about her. Clearly, seeing the lay of the land, I replied, with insincere concern, "How would I get a new library card?"

"We make the forms so simple a first grader can fill them out, but perhaps this was beyond you? Fill out this one-page form, give it to me, and I will send it in. Be sure to give us your correct address. Your new card will arrive in the mail a week to ten days later. That card, Mr. Pace, will be quite different from this ragged, four-year-old card you brought me today." She ripped the old card into pieces and threw into the waste basket. "The new card is modern. It will have a bar code that will keep all of your personal information, and a record of your borrowing and fines. I will only need to swipe it to get those details."

In the face of this up-tight, prim librarian, I could no longer restrain my smart-aleck nature. "Sounds like a remarkable card. Does it send out a little ping if a book is overdue?"

She looked me straight in the eyes, her bright, blue eyes beginning to laugh. "No, Mr. Pace, it does not. But it does emit a brief electrical charge that, for men, can be very uncomfortable." She was really enjoying herself now. "I know what your question is going to be. 'Where does the charge from the card hit on a lady's body?' Well, the answer to that sir, is that ladies do not return books late, and if they do, they pay their fines on time, so there's no need to put the electrical shock mechanism into their cards. Now, do you want the library card or not?"

I said, "I sure do. Any zing like the one you're talking about I can handle with ease."

"Are you sure? Would you bet your library card on it?" Now, she was outright laughing at me.

"Having seen you exercise your authority as the chief librarian, I damned well am going to hold onto my card."

I quickly filled out the application for the new card. She took it, and then, looking at me again, blue eyes mirthfully dancing, she said, "Well, Mr. Pace, I have the authority in extreme cases to cancel fines. And in all my years working as a librarian, I have never met anyone who needs that more than you. So, I welcome you to this wonderful library as a new, *responsible* borrower, knowing that I also have the authority to impose very high fines for delinquencies and even to lock severe delinquents into this library at night so they wander the stacks in the dark forever, like apparitions of long dead Greek gods returning to earth, only to find that they did not land on the sod, but rather on the steel floor of a bibliotheque where, if they move the shelves improperly their necks will be broken."

I don't like to toot my horn as a man who easily gets the attention of women, but even I could figure out that she was flirting with me. "That was beautiful poetic prose that you recited, right off the top of your head. I think I remember in ninth grade English reading that, perhaps in Shakespeare's *Hamlet*, or, more likely, *Mad Magazine*."

She shifted her look in a way that I would learn soon was her "Watch-it-Buster" look.

"Well, I see that my next, most obvious move is to withdraw from the field," I said.

"Yes," she replied. "As fast as you can." She almost sang, her laughter dancing in her eyes.

I left the library and stopped at the curb because the crossing light was red. I stood there, motionless, as if my feet were nailed to the concrete. I stayed as the light changed back and forth, red to green, two times. I couldn't figure out what was going on in my head. Finally, all the pieces fell into place in my soul, and I knew that I had fallen in love with Chief Librarian Virginia Wood—with the same intensity as my love for Dell Bondi. My heart was resurrected.

Somehow, I managed to get myself safely across the street

and into the office. Arleen sat as she usually did, pounding the keys. "Hi Larry," she said. "Where's your book?"

"Well," I began, "I ran into a buzz-saw librarian, who pointed out that my library card had expired three years ago and that I had unpaid fines totaling $25, so she made me apply for a new card and took pity on me and canceled my fines. But, no books until the new card arrives."

Arleen turned in her custom, ergonomic, Arleen chair and spoke in her best, I-am-the- boss tone, "Mr. Pace, when will you get it through your head that I take care of all your personal matters, including your public library use. I will, however, forgive this particular defalcation because you began having your library privileges long before you joined this firm. But, from now on, I will handle your public-library relations. Got it?"

What could I say, being hammered in less than an hour by two powerful women—the one I'd fallen in love with and the one I could not practice law without.

I spent Friday and Saturday and Sunday preparing for a trial in one of the firm's biggest cases. Marty Logue was lead counsel. I was to be his second chair and would also participate in some of the cross examinations. We were already billing the client at a huge rate. If we won, there was certain to be a six-figure final bill. Jury selection was to begin on Wednesday, and the jury pool was huge.

Judge Caffrey, chief judge of the US District Court for the western district of Missouri, was a famous, fast mover, so it was reasonable to believe that jury selection would be completed on Wednesday. Caffrey was well known for continuing the selection process into the evening. If the jury was selected, plaintiffs would have all day Thursday to make their opening statement, and we would have all day Friday to give ours. For the associates completing preparations, Saturday and Sunday would be nearly twenty-four hours per day at work.

On Monday morning, Miss Wood called me to say that the first issues of *Aviation Week* and *Foreign Policy* would arrive on Wednesday. I thanked her and rang off.

Our trial, after nine trial days and lengthy closing arguments resulted in a hung jury. This was a huge result for us because it meant that the plaintiffs would have to try the case all over again if they wanted the kind of money they had hoped for. Our sources had told us that the jury had split seven to five for us, so we had done our job perfectly. The case was teed up for settlement in a small amount.

CHAPTER
5

As was common for trial counsel who had finished a long, emotionally draining case, I took the next week off and stayed with friends, fishing on the Lake of the Ozarks in Missouri. It was a perfect rest that I'd begun even before the sending of the final bill, which would be rendered after the settlement was signed.

When I finally got back to the office, tanned, relaxed, and ready to return to the salt mines, Arleen came in with my mail, opened and sorted perfectly, as it always was. She told me that the librarian had called to say that a book I had long ago requested had finally come in.

Arleen looked at me in her particular way and said, "I don't want you wasting your lunch hour at that library. Your lunch hour is for rest. I'll see that you get that rest here. Oscar will pick up any books from the library and you can read the magazines after hours on the very rare occasions that you will not be working late."

Arleen was nothing but a blunderbuss—straight out of the barrel, full blast. "Your job is to log as many billable hours as you can. My job is to attend to your personal needs, such as seeing that your suits are dry cleaned and delivered here, along with your ironed shirts. I will schedule your medical and dental appointments at the best times for you and the firm."

I felt I should jump in. "And yes," I said sarcastically, "I really appreciated your arranging to have my driveway plowed in the winter. I've been so remiss. I should have thanked you with all my heart, before."

She gave me what I call the "Arleen Look," which, translated, meant "Watch it!"

We gave each other teasingly nasty grins, and I headed back to my office to start grinding on yet another huge money case for the firm.

That case was huge because our client was potentially exposed to a large, punitive damages award. Normally, in a case where someone brings a personal injury or negligence suit, all they get if they win is for actual damages—lost work earnings, medical expenses, pain and suffering, mental distress and that sort of thing—but if the plaintiff shows in addition that the manufacturer was grossly negligent, then the plaintiff may also collect punitive damages, which are not intended to compensate the plaintiff for his loss but rather to punish the defendant. Juries are known to award millions in such cases.

In this case, the plaintiff was suing our client, Great Lakes Lounge Chair, LLC, because the automatic mechanism in the chair, which was supposed to slowly tip forward to assist someone trying to stand up, had malfunctioned. The chair had thrown the plaintiff across the room. He had landed on his head and suffered a concussion, two broken ribs, and a broken left arm.

The company was owned by the only real jerk I had encountered until then—a guy named Morris Podolysky. This idiot had not only mis-designed the lifting mechanism, but he knew it when he offered the chair for sale, and, for reasons known only to his sub-par IQ, he had kept written records clearly showing that the chair was defective and dangerous. He'd also written a memorandum that included the following: "We've already spent too much money on this crappy chair! I don't give a shit whether or not these chairs work. Just start pumping them out and getting them to show-rooms ASAP. Destroy all records of the tests we've run!!"

Fortunately for us, the man's long-suffering secretary, one Rosamond Horton, who had detested him for years, delivered the documents with a copy of her resignation letter to the plaintiff's counsel. The letter read: "I hereby resign immediately, you big, steaming pile of cow turd. It was with the greatest pleasure that I have delivered all of the testing documents to plaintiff's counsel and cashed my bonus check for $100,000, which you signed without looking, when you were yelling at me, 'What are you doing bothering me now with all this paper work. I should'a gotten rid of you years ago!'"

Podolysky, like all manufacturers, had substantial liability insurance that would pay the likely damages verdict in its entirety. The insurance company had hired us to defend Podolysky and his company in the negligence suit, but Podolysky was our actual client.

Even experienced litigators like Marty Logue and others in the firm were appalled by Podolysky's irresponsibility toward the public. Jaded attorneys, they were nonetheless dismayed by his willful choice to send the dangerous chair to market, and they were astounded by the written records he kept. Still, insurance defense work is good money. It fills the gaps in income that periodically torment all law firms and is especially prized because the insurance companies' checks never bounce.

In terms of this case, one problem was that Podolysky had lots of assets sprinkled over seven or eight midwestern states, some held personally, but the majority held by shell corporations. In most law suits, if you can show at the outset a high likelihood of success, you can get a court order putting a lien on the property of the defendant so that it will be available to pay any judgement. This order is commonly called an "attachment," but for this approach to work in our case, certified copies of the attachment order had to be filed in the land or personal property records of the state or the county where Podolysky's property was located. Some states might require the plaintiff to file a law suit in that state, under the full faith and credit provision of the Constitution.

In Podolysky's case, our research had already identified ten states where he or an entity he controlled had assets. Obviously, the process of recording the attachments in the relevant state or county records would be extremely expensive, but Oscar, who knew all about this stuff, could help.

We could handle the logistics of the attachments, but there was one issue. The plaintiff's lawyer was young and inexperienced and he had omitted a claim for punitive damages in his complaint. We decided to give him a little help. I went to Arleen, who in turn went to Oscar, who in turn showed up at the young attorney's office, offering him his detective services, while at the same time gently pointing out his omission.

Some of you are now saying, "Aren't you committing a violation of legal ethics if you help a plaintiff when you already represent the defendant?" Our Ethics Committee in the firm asked the same question, and our answer was simple: "We had only represented Podolysky against the claims for actual damages. His insurance policy did not cover punitive damages, and he had never retained us to represent him on those claims, so, where was the conflict?" Our Ethics Committee bought it, and Marty Logue handed this hot potato to me, saying, "Larry, you get that son of a bitch!"

And I did. The jury quickly came back with a plaintiff's verdict, awarding $10,000 in actual damages, another $100,000 in pain and suffering, and $500,000 in punitive damages. When the final judgement was issued, Marty came into my office, stuck his hand out and said, "Superb job, Larry. All of us are pleased to have you as a member of our firm."

CHAPTER

6

Marty's thanks clearly carried with it the message that a senior partnership was on the horizon. With this little nugget in mind, I pounded away, sometimes generating up to fifteen billable hours daily.

Unbeknownst to me, Miss Wood and Arleen, who by now were acquainted with one another because of all the books and magazines I'd ordered, had had lunch together. As I learned later, Miss Wood had wanted to know specifically whether or not Arleen felt I was a good man, because, as she had explained to Arleen, she wanted lots of children. At twenty-seven, her clock was ticking, and she wanted very much to get married as soon as possible. Arleen's reply was, "He's a great guy. He got dumped a while back by someone he deeply loved, but I think he's pretty much over that." After pausing for ten seconds, Arleen had added, "And I think you would be a good couple." She handed Miss Wood her card, with my home phone number written on the back.

When I picked up my home phone at about 9:30 that night, I heard, "Hi Larry. This is Virginia Wood—Ginny."

Then a pause. For a brief moment, I had no idea who she was. She quickly went on, "I'm the librarian. The books and magazine woman?"

"Oh," I said. "Certainly, I remember."

She quickly went on, nervously. "I don't know if Arleen has told you about our new service. We are now open until 9:00 pm every weekday, so it will be much more convenient for you to get the magazines and books that you want."

"Well that's great. I'm so glad you called," I said. This was followed by silence, and then more silence, until suddenly the pieces came clearly together in my mind. Now was the time to ask this lady on a date, so I said, "How about we have dinner some night?"

She perked up and said with great enthusiasm, "Oh sure!"

"How about dinner this Friday at the Savoy Grill?"

She replied, "That sounds just fine. I love that place. How about meeting there at six o'clock or so?"

That remark made it clear that she had no intention of letting me drive her anywhere that evening. Dinner would just be a meet-and-greet in a crowded, noisy restaurant.

I got a reservation and arrived at the Savoy that Friday a few minutes before six. I was just sliding into the booth when I saw Ginny come through the door, wearing an attractive dress of blue, pink, and yellow that hung loosely from her shoulders to her ankles.

I stood up as she approached the booth. She slid in across from me. When the waiter came, I ordered an ounce of Scotch with a small bottle of soda on the side. Ginny got a Pinot Grigio. We settled back, enjoying our drinks, and started talking. I don't remember whether or not our meals were any good, but I do remember that our conversation started with the drinks and continued until past the end of dessert. We meandered back and forth covering a variety of subjects, laughing as we went.

I talked about growing up in Rochester, New York. After the war, my dad remained in Germany for seven months and was paid in Allied Occupation Marks, the currency of the occupation. When he mustered out, my dad was amazed to learn that he would be paid one dollar for each mark. In his case, this came to four thousand dollars, which he used to buy our first home at 184 Croyden Road. Most of the men around us were like my father. They'd come home from the war and wanted to start families, so our neighborhood was filled with kids.

I told Ginny how much fun we had playing hide-and-seek. We made the big oak tree in our yard the It-Spot, from which we fanned out to find hiding places. One Saturday afternoon, when seven or eight of us were playing, I hid behind some of the beautifully manicured bushes in front of the Jones' house, next door to ours. Mr. and Mrs. Jones were an older, childless couple, who stayed distant from us kids. At one point in the midst of the game that day, for some reason still unknown to me, I felt it was a good idea to stand up slowly and look through the living room window, where Mrs. Jones was knitting and talking with her husband. When she saw me, she bolted upright, dropped her knitting, and shrieked, "Lee! Lee! It's a peeping Tom!" I fled in terror for the It-Tree.

The Jones' doted on two things: their beautifully tended lawn and their great cars. They bought a new car every year, which was quite common in those days. Mr. Jones always got the most expensive models of the Cadillac Fleetwood sedan, while Mrs. Jones preferred two-door, bright blue Lincoln Continentals.

My sister had her own tangle with the Jones'. She had a good friend, Margot. Together, they were always getting into some kind of mischief. One day, when Mr. Jones drove his brand new Caddy into the driveway, the girls each picked up a handful of gravel and threw it at his glistening car. They threw so hard that I saw little chips of paint fly off. When my father heard what they'd done, he was so angry that he actually spanked my sister—something he'd never done to either of us in all of our childhood. Their mischief had made us bad neighbors, but it also caused Mr. Jones to submit a bill for the re-painting of his car.

Ginny told me many fun stories, too, about her learning to ride, falling off horses, and her family's trips to the county fair. Finally, at eleven o'clock, when she said it was time for her to leave. I only remember two things: being drawn to her by a certain *je ne sais quoi* and learning that she, like I, loved line dancing. "Wait a minute," I said. "How about doing some line dancing next Friday?"

She paused and replied, "Well, I have other plans." But she remained at the table, looking at me.

"How about Saturday night?" I asked.

She smiled. "I could do it then. There's a great dance up at the Palisades in North KC starting at seven."

I was about to say, "I will meet you there then," but she suggested, "How about if I meet you there at 5:30 and we have dinner first."

I jumped at it. "That's a great idea. There's a restaurant there called Cattleman's Italian Restaurant. It has every kind of beef and Italian dish, including 101 pizzas, which we're going to need if we're going to do some hard clomping."

"Meet you at the restaurant no later than 5:30. We can't be late for all the dancing," she warned.

When I got into bed that night, I wondered. *What's going on? I don't even know her. But being with her feels right.* And within seconds, I was sound asleep.

CHAPTER
7

Saturday evening, I put on my outfit—a white, Western-style shirt, tight jeans, and a hand-tooled, leather belt with a worked silver buckle (not the big, pretentious oval that some folks wear). I slipped into my made-to-order Lucchese boots and stood in front of my full-length mirror for a minute or two, admiring myself.

I slipped behind the wheel of my Mercedes and headed north for the big dance. When I walked into the restaurant, I saw Ginny seated in a booth way in the back. The place was already jammed with a boisterous crowd. As I headed toward her, she paid no attention, then, doing a double take, she stared at me and slid out of the booth. We each checked each other's outfits out. After a second or two, she held up both thumbs and started toward me.

I was stunned by her appearance. She did a slow pirouette, giving me plenty of time to appreciate her well-rounded, enticing derriere. Her shirt, a perfectly pressed, scorching pink, had blue fringe down the arms, matching the color of her jeans, and piping running across her chest, looping up over one breast and down, then over the other breast and down. I quickly noticed that the Mother of Pearl snaps on her shirt were unsnapped low enough to reveal a flicker of cleavage.

Ginny started toward me, her hips sliding back and forth, with her arms out, making me think that she was going to give me a close hug. Instead she placed her right hand firmly against my chest to maintain our distance. With her other hand on my shoulder, she whispered in my ear, "That cheap belt buckle—I don't know—it's definitely not line-dancing quality. I'm afraid they're not even going to let you into the dance."

Ginny backed off, pointing to her buckle. I looked at the buckle and at her, and said, "If you want to unbuckle it, it's fine with me." She stared at me, her face neither happy nor sad, but clearly taking me in. Then, softly and slowly, she said, "I think there's a long row to hoe before anything like that ever happens. I'll just make sure they don't keep us out because of that buckle," and she slid into the booth.

I told her how great she looked, and she said, "Apart from your cheesy belt buckle, you're one of the best looking guys I've ever seen."

That burying of the hatchet resulted in our having a marvelous dinner. We sat listening to a wonderful piano player and the uproarious laughter from the packed bar. The harried waiters were almost sprinting from table to table. Ginny ordered a Mustard Cat Fish Splendor and I had grilled pork chops stuffed with a mango sauce. We each decided to have iced tea instead of liquor, so we would be on our toes for the big dance.

When we finished dinner, we got up and headed for the

dance barn. As we approached, we could hear the music and the noise, and by the time we got inside, we saw an incredible bash—people drinking at the bar, dancing with anyone, and as the evening wore, on drunkards falling on the floor.

But it was the dancing that I will never forget. She was a fantastic dancer, with all the right moves—as I was. We danced with each other and also lots of other guys and gals looking for a partner or a line to join. The music from the live band—fiddle, guitar, banjo, and, of all things, a trumpet—just boiled the blood with excitement.

After three and a half hours, exhausted dancers started to stagger out of the barn, although several were drunk in the corners and likely would not make it home. As we walked to my car in the parking lot, Ginny gently slid her right arm through my left arm and leaned softly against me, until we got to my Mercedes. She ogled the car and asked, "Where did you get such a car?" I mumbled something about its being from the firm and asked her where her car was. She said, "Right here," pointing to the old VW van parked next to mine.

"That's your car?" I exclaimed.

"Yes," she replied.

It was my turn to stare at her. She turned to me, holding my hand, and said, "Thank you so much for a marvelous evening."

"I had a great time too," I said. "Let's do it again soon."

Walking toward her car, she looked back and said, "We'll see." And with that, she turned smartly on the heel of her custom-made boot, climbed into the driver's seat, and started the engine. The car obviously needed a full exhaust replacement, but she started chugging down the road after she blew me a kiss. I watched her until her tail lights disappeared, knowing for certain that I had fallen hard for Virginia Wood, the hard-hearted, take-no-prisoners, fine-enforcing chief librarian, who could, nonetheless, blow a guy like me a kiss.

CHAPTER
8

For the next weeks, I was jammed with work and stayed in the office until at least nine, and sometimes much later, working on cases for what was now four big insurance company defendants, racking up huge fees, minute by minute. That is the way things are at law offices—not much work one day and twenty-four-hours a day the next. Arleen understood this perfectly and was with me the whole way, doing the hardest work, getting the word processing correctly finalized, and otherwise preparing drafts of what would be documents for very important to the cases.

At the beginning of the third week, when things had cooled down, Arleen, in a certain, tender tone, said, "You know, the lady at the library called to let me know that the magazines that you like are in." After a brief pause, she added, "I told her you were working much too hard and would not be able to come to the library for two weeks. I said you'd come during your lunch hour sometime."

Now, I may be stupid, but I am not dumb, and I picked up the obvious change Arleen had made to my library practices—I was invited to get my library materials during my lunch hour, not after hours. *So,* I thought to myself, *In addition to other talents, Arleen is a matchmaker.*

On the Monday when I was finally done with the back-breaking work of the past several weeks, I headed across the street to the library. I stopped as I looked across the corridor to the desk where Ginny was handing a book to a borrower. Her auburn hair gleamed in the ceiling lights and her tense conversation with the borrower, interspersed with occasional laughter, made my heart rate climb to near heart attack level. I knew that I had fallen heavily for the librarian. I loved her now, in every corner of my soul.

Somehow, despite my sudden feelings of love, I was able to make it to the front of the desk. I don't think she saw me until I got there. She was bending down looking for something underneath and stood up, pausing for a moment and then said, "Hi there, dancing guy. Do you want to take out a book?"

"No," I replied. "I'd like to take out you!"

She looked stunned and fidgeted with her hands, then said, stuttering a little, "What do you have in mind?"

"Well," I said, "I'm sure you know that the Nelson Art Gallery is open on Saturdays. I'd like to have lunch there with you, and then take a look at whatever they've got exhibited now. How about it?"

She seemed startled and looked nervous and a little shy. Her eyes widened and she fiddled with a pencil. Then, in an intensely wary tone, she replied, "I could meet you there for lunch on the patio."

"How about noon?" I asked.

Chapter 8

Again. she paused and finally said, "I think that will work."

"Great. See you then!" I turned, with my heart pounding as I walked quickly to the door. I did not realize until I got outside, to the edge of the road, that I had not inquired about the magazines. No matter. There were only four days until I would see her again at the Nelson.

CHAPTER

9

It was a beautiful, cobalt blue afternoon when the two of us sat down for lunch on the outside patio of the Nelson. The patio restaurant is known for its terrific food and our lunches were just that. As we ate, we chatted aimlessly until the assistant manager of the museum came over to tell me that the docent I had reserved to be with us had called in sick and that he had no replacement. He apologized profusely, saying, "This has never happened before!"

We were on our own, so we headed out into the wilds of the Nelson Art Gallery. As we walked to the first exhibit room, Ginny turned to me, and said, "You know, I know a lot about art of all kinds. I minored in art history at K.U. because my advisor thought the field would fit well with my library studies."

I was stunned. "At Haverford, I majored in Eastern European history with a minor in art history!"

She gaped at me, and I thought I saw a flicker of deeper interest, as if she had just checked off another box.

For the rest of the afternoon, we strolled the magnificent

galleries, talking about brush strokes, painters like Van Gogh who made works of stunning brightness, and the portraits by the Dutch masters so carefully done that they appeared to be photographs.

That afternoon, when we parted, I noted that the exhaust system on her VW had been repaired.

CHAPTER
10

Every year, in Omaha, Nebraska, there is a month-long horse racing extravaganza, commonly called the Ak-Sar-Ben Races. I knew of them because of my Uncle Alan.

Uncle Alan lives in a little town in New York called Irondequoit, near Rochester. He is by far the wealthiest of my father and his brothers. He is also the biggest tightwad in the family. When he pulls a dollar bill out of his wallet, he presses it between his thumb and finger, smoothing it several times to make sure that he is handing over only one bill.

For years, Alan had been a farmer and had also raised sulky horses and racing horses. In the mid-fifties, he sold his place for $500,000 to a huge developer who wanted to build a shopping center. Alan, who loved his horses, refused to sell the whole parcel and reserved thirty acres, including his barns, for his horses, whom he loved as if they were his children. He and his wife Sonia were childless.

Alan raced his sulkies and his thoroughbreds at the huge Finger Lakes Racetrack, almost always betting on one or more of the horses he owned. His thoroughbreds were not of

Triple Crown status, but they were well worth racing in lesser venues, and he did so regularly. He himself was a superb rider. When I watched him ride, it was as if he and his horse were almost in love with each other.

About two weeks after Ginny and I had lunch at the Nelson, I got a letter from Alan reminding me that he would be at Ak-Sar-Ben this year. He asked if I could come to watch the races and say hello. I carefully pondered the invitation, largely wondering how I could invite Ginny. Obviously, we would be taking my Mercedes because it would be foolish to take two cars, and even more foolish to take her ten-year-old, sputtering VW bus. We would be there for two nights, so the issue was our sleeping arrangements.

I called and made a reservation for two separate rooms at one of the motels near the track. That evening after work, I went to the library, ostensibly to read my magazines, though when I saw Ginny, I said hello and quickly invited her to join me at the races. I told her that I hoped she would come. My guess had been that she would tell me she'd call in a couple of days after she'd thought it over, but all she said was "Boy, that's exciting! I've never seen a horse race. Would we need to stay overnight?"

"Yes, for two nights. And I have already made reservations for two separate rooms at a motel up there. No problem if you don't want to come. I can easily cancel one."

"No, I'd love to come," she said. "It sounds exciting. But we'll only need one car. It's probably not a good idea to take my VW."

To which I replied, "Never in a million years. We'll cruise up there in the Mercedes."

We each arranged to leave work early that Friday. I picked her up at her condo and we headed north. The drive across

50

Kansas and Nebraska to Omaha was stunning—flat, full of huge farms, horrifically expensive farm equipment, and friendly faces. We got to the motel at about 6:30 and checked in, only to find that there was one room available, not two. "I cannot tell you how much I regret this, sir," the owner said, "but though you made reservations for two rooms, you only confirmed for one." Ginny looked uncomfortable and I was increasingly upset, until I looked at him sternly, "No, I confirmed for two. I sent you a letter!"

The man looked puzzled, but I figured out pretty quickly what was going on. There were no "single rooms," only "double rooms," and he stuck us in one room to free up another for at least four guests. Motel space was short, and he wanted to make more money.

I went out to the car to get our luggage, and when I got back, the owner told me that Ginny had gone to the room ahead of me. He handed me my key. I went to the room and discovered that it was in fact a single, with only one double bed. I briefly panicked, because I knew that this would not do for Ginny, but then I saw that she was already resolving the problem. Parked in the far corner was a fold up, rollaway bed. She was stringing clothesline across the room, tying it to lamp fixtures on the wall. She threw a large blanket over the line and shoved the rollaway bed into the room she'd created, unlatching it, and covering it with sheets and a blanket. She added a pillow. It was clear that she had not been idle.

"Boy, this is just like Clark Gable and Claudette Colbert in *It Happened One Night*," I said.

Ginny gave me an arched look and replied, "Actually not, because the walls of Jericho are not coming down!"

Ginny asked me to step over to the space she'd created and said, "This is your room," looking at me as if to say, "You screwed it up. You sleep here."

We ate dinner at a restaurant just down the street from the motel. Ginny ordered spinach ravioli covered with cheese sauce and capers. I had bouillabaisse stew, which I love, and which was, frankly, one of the best I'd ever had. The good food and a split of Pinot Grigio quieted any bad feelings we might have had because of the room screw up.

When we got back to the motel, I offered to shower first. I also wanted to shave because I hadn't that morning. The problem was that after I had taken off all of my clothing in the bathroom and bathed and shaved, I had to put my clothes back on again to walk past Ginny's bed to get to my "room." This was an annoyance, but actually not that big a deal. Because I'd thought that we'd each have our own room, I hadn't brought pajamas, so I took off my pants and lay down in my underwear and shirt. The bed was remarkably comfortable. Ginny had moved a standing lamp and put it near the head of my bed. She'd placed a Gideon Bible on my pillow. As I looked at it, I pondered the possible meaning of that gift.

After she showered, I assume that Ginny got into her nightgown and walked back to her bed. She turned on the light. When I glanced at her beyond the edge of the blanket, I saw that she was reading and asked, "Is it a good book? What's it about?"

She turned toward my "room" and said, "I normally don't talk when I'm reading."

I lay back and drifted off into a deep sleep. It had been a long and exhausting day.

CHAPTER
11

Ginny awakened me early in the morning by tickling my feet and offering me a large cup of black coffee. We agreed we had each slept well, and we talked about the day to come.

"I think we should scout out your Uncle Alan first. Neither of us a whole lot about horse racing," she suggested.

I agreed, so we hopped into my Mercedes and headed to the race track. This was the first day of the racing schedule, and the parking lot was jammed with cars, horse trailers, and pickups. Some people were tailgating their breakfasts. We followed others who were heading for the paddocks.

I saw Uncle Alan immediately, grooming his beautiful, black mare and hosing her down. I yelled his name. He turned and lit up with a big smile. Alan is one of the happiest people I've ever met. Things just seemed to him to be going swimmingly, no matter what the disaster. He turned off the hose, handed the halter to the groom, and jogged over yelling, "By God, it's Larry! You've made it. I was getting afraid we wouldn't see you!"

I gave him a big hug and told him how happy I was to see him. "Where's Sonia?" I asked.

"She's back in the mobile home over there," he said, pointing to a huge ocean liner on wheels at the end of the parking area. When I say huge, I mean that it was like a two-bedroom, luxury house—the type of accommodation that has always been Alan's preference.

As Alan pointed, Sonia came out and down the steps. Alan waved her over. She spryly sprinted across the parking lot between the cars and shortly was in front of me, standing on her tip toes and hugging me as hard as she could while mumbling in my ear, "Oh Larry, we're so glad you came. I think Alan's got a real winner here. We should do quite well in the dollar department!"

Alan and Sonia had much the same view of money: they wanted lots of it and didn't want to spend it, except on matters related to horses and certain areas pertaining to their own comfort.

Alan turned to me. "Where are you parked?" he asked. I pointed to the car, and he said approvingly, "That's a pretty fine one you've got there, Larry. I think a current-year Mercedes, top of the line, is very, very expensive! How did a poor lawyer like you ever afford such a thing?"

"Well, Uncle, it's just a perk of my job. I don't own it. It's leased. But I did get to choose the model, the color, and the interior. It is one road-eating wonder!"

Alan then turned his attention to Ginny. (You had to know Alan to understand that a beautiful car would always come before a beautiful woman.) "Well, and you, young lady. You're a lovely person. I'm Alan."

Chapter 11

Before I could answer, Ginny stepped up and introduced herself, saying that I had invited her to come see a horse race. "I've never seen one before," she said. "It's very exciting. And I am amazed at the size of the horses. They are just huge!"

Alan ate this up. "Well, follow me," he said, "and I will show you huge horses, truly beautiful animals." He took Ginny's hand and we followed Alan and Sonia down to the paddock. They introduced us to the groom, who, Alan was careful to say, was vital to racing success because he knew how to take care of the horses. "Like Rainbow, here," he said, pointing to the enormous black mare."

Sonia asked if we'd like breakfast, and we both responded with a simultaneous yes. I was starving, and Ginny was, too. "I've got a great breakfast in our Land Whale, so come with me," Sonia urged.

As we walked behind them, Ginny slipped her arm through mine and whispered, "I love her dress. Does she sew?"

"Oh yeah," I said. "She loves to sew, but she'll only use her old Singer—no Viking or super modern machines."

"Well," Ginny said. "I would really love to see that machine."

We got to the Land Whale and went in. It was huge. Beyond the driver's seat there was a kitchenette, and beyond that, a luxurious sitting area with tinted windows and leather furniture. It was about the size of a small living room in a home. Beyond that, we could see a little of the bedroom, with its queen-size bed covered by a multi-colored, hand-woven bedspread. Ginny stepped forward immediately and reached down to run her fingers across the tightly woven fabric. She turned to Sonia and said, "I'll bet you have your own loom!"

Sonia threw back her head and laughed. "I certainly do, but Alan and I have never figured out a way to take it with us in the Land Whale, so when we get home to Irondequoit, I just sprint upstairs to slake my thirst for weaving. I've got three looms."

At this point, Alan, stepped in and reminded her, "Dearest, breakfast!"

Sonia clapped her hands and went to the stove, where everything was all set. She served shirred eggs, blueberry muffins, cold salami, newly cooked bacon, and several kinds of cereals and juices. We all dug in, and for a while, no one spoke. We savored the taste and scent of the carefully prepared, welcome breakfast.

As we stood up to leave, I motioned to Sonia. She came near me, and I bent over and whispered in her ear, "Auntie, I need a pair of pajamas."

With a sly twinkle in her eye, she said, "Choose from this drawer full," after she led me to the bedroom, where, unbeknownst to Uncle Alan, I purloined a set of his pajamas, which, it turned out, I have to this day.

CHAPTER
12

Ginny and I had planned to leave early on Sunday morning, but we had enjoyed Alan and Sonia so much and they made very clear that they wanted us to have another breakfast with them, so we stayed, talking, and laughing. Sonia was good at telling off-color jokes, and she told a few of them. Before we knew it, it was lunchtime.

We really did have to skeedaddle, so we all hugged each other, and as I turned to go, Alan got a big, ingratiating smile on his face and said something that I knew he would say at some point, "Larry, how 'bout I take a little spin in that Mercedes?" How could I possibly have said no? I handed him the keys. "Hop in, Sonia," he said, "I want to see if this thing is even half worth the ninety grand it costs to buy!"

To which Sonia replied, "Alan, like all of the Paces, you are an unnecessary skin flint! I have told you this for years, and I'm telling you again. If you want one of these over-priced, foreign cars, then get one for the funeral business and deduct the damn thing!"

Ginny looked at me quizzically. "What funeral business?"

Alan piped right up. "Well, I'm in the undertaking business because there's *never* a shortage of bodies needing embalmment and burial, while with the horse business, well, that's another story. Horses are expensive. Real expensive. And I just can't give them up."

My aunt turned to Ginny and further explained, "Alan has been breeding both race horses and sulky horses. Do you know what those are?"

Ginny replied, "Not really. What's a sulky?"

My aunt explained, "Well, it's used in a kind of racing that is quite popular where we come from. Basically, it's a small, two-wheeled open cart that's drawn by a horse and driven by a rider sitting inside it. Sulky races are extremely fast and competitive. They remind me of the chariot race in the movie *Ben Hur,* with Charlton Heston, if you've ever seen that."

I knew that Ginny, as a west Kansas farm girl, had never seen or heard of *Ben Hur,* or, very possibly Charlton Heston, but she did get the general idea of sulky racing.

"We do this racing at a place called the Finger Lakes Racetrack in western New York state, where we live," Sonia continued. "If you know what you're doing, and believe me we do" you can make lots of money betting on sulky races! Maybe sometime, Larry, you'd like to bring this lovely lady to visit? We'll take her down there. How about that?"

Ginny replied, "I'd just love to visit you sometime, Sonia. You've been so kind."

To which Sonia replied, "You come and we'll get you in a sulky. You'll love it. And I'll bet you'll win us all lots of money!"

Ginny responded with an odd, confused look, no doubt

trying to cope with two Kansas farm girl no-no's: horse races and betting on them. To say nothing of the tease that she, or anyone else, could quickly learn to drive a sulky.

Alan would not be deterred from the Mercedes, so, with a slightly scolding tone, he said to Sonia, "Hop in, we're going for a drive," and off they went, through the parking lot and out.

One of Alan's least attractive personality traits is that he rarely concerns himself with the needs of living people, except when he has to, so they took their time cruising around in my Mercedes and did not get back for about half an hour. As they got out of the car, I heard Sonia say, "Alan, this is a piece of junk! We've got to stick to our Cadillacs, because Cadillac makes hearses as well as cars. Two for the price of one!"

Alan did not reply verbally but he had a look on his face that I've known since I was a kid: his way or the embalming table. Cadillacs it was. At any rate, finally, it was time to go. After warm hugs, we got in the Mercedes and headed home.

After we had waved goodbye one last time, Ginny looked at me and said, "Larry, thank you so for inviting me, not only to these races. Thanks for giving me the chance to meet members of your family. Alan and Sonia are," and she paused, then continued, "interesting people. Right?"

"You could say that," I said, "but they're caring and true family members. It's not just Alan who's the tight wad. It's Sonia as well."

As we drove, I enjoyed the car as much as ever. Ginny was silent, though, apparently thinking deeply. "You know," she said, "I've always wanted to have a family. How do you feel about those kinds of things?"

Somewhere, in my soul, I felt a tingle. We turned to each

other briefly, then I looked back at the road and said, "I think I'd like a family. At least, I have imagined that, but I'm not so sure how I would actually be as a parent. I mean, kids can be a real pain!"

We were quiet for the next five miles or so, and then Ginny said softly, looking at me, "You're right, of course, but making and caring for a family is at least a full-time, two-person job, wouldn't you say?"

After another five miles or so, I replied, "Well, there would be the issue of the walls of Jericho coming down, wouldn't you say?"

After another five miles, Ginny spoke softly, "Larry, the walls of Jericho will fall one nanosecond after I'm married!"

"I get that," I said.

CHAPTER
13

The next three weeks at the office were another madhouse of work—a get-everything-done-yesterday period of time, as is often the case in a busy law office. I would later learn that Arleen, whose goal in life is to know everything about everyone, had somehow divined that Ginny and I were dating, and, of course, she spoke to Ginny about me. Arleen made clear to Ginny how busy I was, which I am sure, conveyed the clear message that I had not forgotten about her nor was I ignoring her, though I was not in much contact with her.

For me, this burst of work was related to what would become one the firm's most celebrated and lucrative cases. Unusually for us, we were representing a plaintiff, the Central States Oil and Gas Corporation and its subsidiary, Central States Drilling, Inc. Almost unheard of at our firm, we had taken the case for a contingency fee of 30 percent of the gross recovery, in addition to our expenses. This was a gamble, of course, because if we lost we would recover nothing: for the hundreds of hours we'd put in, no recompense. If we won, the reward for the firm would be tremendous.

The two companies routinely drilled oil and natural gas wells. To make this possible, they bought leases from landowners, paying the owners a percentage of the profits. The companies initially hired our firm to look into concerns that they were not getting all of the oil and gas they were entitled to.

This, of course, meant that Oscar was on the scene, doing his exemplary detective work. His final report and its appendix of supporting documents made clear that many of the landowners had drilled into the ground to tap the oil and gas before it was recovered from the well. This is called "angle ironing." Oscar had somehow obtained secret, internal documents that showed that our clients had been deprived of profits of nearly $150 million. Because representing these clients meant high expenses and complicated jury trials, I was made chief counsel.

The cases went to trial about three months after Ginny and I got back from Ak-Sar-Ben. Preparations consumed virtually all of my time and energy, and frankly, were the cause of great stress. In fact, although I had the full resources of the firm behind me, in the end, it was Arleen who made it all work, not just because of her skilled document preparation, but because of how, by talking with me gently or sometimes putting her hand on my shoulder, she allayed the immense anxiety I had about being in charge of these huge cases.

In the end, pre-trial, we had gotten attachments, which are liens on defendants' properties that forbid transfer. If we won, there would be lots of assets to satisfy the judgements. Thanks to Oscar's work, and, long story short, after the functional equivalent of the Third World War, we won every-thing—$250 million for both regular and punitive damages.

It took several years before all the appeals were exhausted, but we ultimately prevailed. Then, as is always the case in the legal game, we had the challenge of collecting. Again, this was where Oscar came in. We had hundreds of landown-ers and companies that had cheated our clients. Each had assets, including bank accounts and machinery, wherever their operations were located. It took many, many years, but thanks to Oscar's research, we recovered every dime that was owed, including the 10 percent interest that was accruing on the unpaid portions.

Once we had gotten the final judgement, before the actual hearing of the appeals began, my job had been pretty much done. When the judgement was finally upheld on appeal and we'd begun collecting, there was nothing more for me to do, and in any case, I was so exhausted I probably could not have done anything more.

Arleen saw to my getting a hefty month of vacation. I had done the best I could to keep in touch with Ginny as I was working on the case. She occasionally called me late at night or at work, and I always took a few minutes to talk. I was too tired to go anywhere, but Ginny came to visit some-times. Looking back after it was over, I realized that even as I was working literally eighteen-hour days, those occasional moments with her had shown me that she was kind and understanding, and I fell more deeply in love with her.

Once I had fully recovered, Ginny said, "Look, you've got lots of time off now, and I can take a couple of days off. Why don't we head out to western Kansas, and I'll introduce you to my family? I know they aren't as colorful as your Uncle Alan—none of them are funeral directors—but they are really nice people.

Of course, I said yes, but with the proviso that we take my car, not her thundering VW bus. Ginny had gotten to appreciate the comfortable leather seating in the Mercedes and the quietness of its ride, so there was no dispute: her VW would remain in her garage. And mid-morning one Friday, we hopped onto I-70, then a two-lane road, and headed for Salinas, Kansas.

CHAPTER
14

To call western Kansas flat does a service to your average pancake. The flat prairie extends all the way across eastern Colorado to the Rocky Mountains, which, in the distance, appear as silver peaks on the horizon. Salina cannot claim to anything that's physically appealing, but as it turned out, it can claim to be the home of the marvelous Wood family.

Ginny had obviously prepped her family for this visit. I would later learn that they were in a vise. On the one hand, they remembered with pain and sorrow the number of proposals she had turned down, from when she was eighteen to the present, when she was twenty-nine. She had refused twelve. On the other hand, they did not want her to marry any kind of jerk.

As we pulled into the long, gravel driveway leading to her family's old farmhouse, we were greeted by what I later learned was her entire living family, from her great grandmother, who was one hundred and two, to her niece Annie, who was six months old. The adults knew I was a lawyer, which was good because that would spare me rounds and rounds of lawyer jokes. The Mercedes was also probably helpful to my cause.

As we got out of the car and walked toward them, the family surged around us. Ginny introduced me to her mom and dad, Russell and Jaclyn. They in turn introduced me to everyone else, including Annie. Truth be told, I was deeply moved by their greeting. It was filled with warmth and affection and palpable relief that Ginny had finally hooked a man she might actually agree to marry. They treated me as one of the family from the moment I got out of the car.

I was very impressed with her father as a businessman. He had to be good to be successful because, I was surprised to learn, he did not breed and sell cattle. He ran an auction house where others could buy and sell their animals. Later, he gave me a hilarious example of the almost incomprehensible language used by auctioneers to recognize one bid, then a higher one, and so on.

Saturday was filled with sightseeing—cattle, tractors, auction houses. We had a great time. On Sunday, we intended to leave early in the morning, but the goodbyes went on for a good while. We ended up eating breakfast and left a little before noon.

On I-70, as we clicked along at nearly eighty miles an hour, Ginny asked me what I thought of her family. "I think they are wonderful!" I said. "There was a lot of genuine love among them. I hope *my* family will seem the same to you."

Ginny took my hand gently and said, "No doubt in my mind. How could any family that includes Alan and Sonia be anything but a blast?"

We both started laughing. Little did she know.

CHAPTER
15

The next issue for Ginny and me was getting to my parents' home in Rochester. This turned out to be challenging, partly because the law grind for the next couple of months was very heavy, with lots of firm fees at stake. Finally, we were able to identify a long weekend when we could go. With my family forewarned and eager for our visit, we flew from Kansas City, changed planes at Pittsburgh, and landed in Rochester at nine in the evening.

My parents, Jason and Mildred Pace, stood at the airport gate to greet us. They were overjoyed to see us both get off the plane. Like Ginny's family, they worried about my prospects for marriage. My mother in particular knew of my heartache over Dell's disappearance and had been kind and reassuring to me.

My father extended his big hand to Ginny and as she took it, pulled her to him, looked her in the eyes, and said, "As usual, Larry understated and didn't express even half of how lovely you are. It is such a pleasure to meet you!" With the huge grin on his face revealing his lily-white dentures, he added again, "It's just wonderful to meet you!" My mother stepped up and took Ginny by both hands. She said much the same thing in her winning and welcoming tone, which told me that she liked Ginny immediately.

My father picked up Ginny's suitcase and I carried mine as we walked toward my parents' car. When we got to there, I noticed that they no longer had their old eight-hole Buick Roadmaster but had instead graduated to a Cadillac Fleetwood, four-door sedan—dark blue with a matching leather interior. A beauty! In those days, General Motors produced five cars: Chevrolet, Pontiac, Oldsmobile, Buick, and Cadillac. GM marketed the cars as a way to demonstrate to all concerned that one had moved up the ladder of success if one started with a Chevrolet and ended with a Cadillac.

I can still remember the day my parents drove home in their Buick Roadmaster. It was gray on the bottom and white on the top, with four holes on each side of the hood. The holes indicated the number of cylinders in the engine, identifying the model of the car. As a child, I was so taken with that Buick I used to carry my dinner out of the house and into the car, where I sat quietly and enjoyed its ambiance.

My father opened the trunk of the Cadillac, which appeared to be the size of a living room, and carefully placed our luggage there, avoiding any chance of damage to his new car. My mother held open one rear door and invited Ginny to climb in. My mother followed her. My father slipped into the driver's seat, I took the other front seat, and we were off. By this time, it was dusk, and when we reached my parents' home on Edgemere Drive, on Lake Ontario, night had fallen.

I have always enjoyed returning to my parents' magnificent home, with its brick walls and slate roof. It had two full floors, a large kitchen and dining room that both overlooked the lake, a winterized porch, five bedrooms (each with a full bath), and a library on the second floor.

My mother had prepared a light supper, which we ate sitting at my parents' huge Victorian-style dining table. Dinner was vintage Mom, prepared in just the amount right for a late evening meal before bed: corn on the cob, steamed beets, trout pan fried in lemon butter, and a chilled bottle of Sauvignon Blanc. Near the end of the meal, Ginny yawned. My mother observed this and led us both up to our bedrooms. Ginny's room was at the far corner, just to the right of the top of the stairs, with windows on two sides, now blackened by night. Mother showed her to the bathroom and encouraged her to use the chest of drawers and closet. I walked across the hall to the bedroom that had always been mine: one double bed and an attached shower.

Before I got into bed, I donned the notorious pair of Uncle Alan's pajamas that Aunt Sonia had given me and knocked on Ginny's door. She opened it with both a smile and an expression of obvious fatigue. "You are so fortunate to have the parents you have," she said. "Their warm welcome was so thoughtful and kind. I think there has been a lot of love in this home—always a good thing." She leaned forward, hugged me hard for just a moment, told me to sleep well, and said goodnight, but only after lightly reminding me that the Walls of Jericho were still not coming down.

My mother was up early the next morning, preparing for breakfast and the huge family gathering that was planned for me and Ginny. At about 6:30, I heard someone knocking on my door with great urgency. Bang, bang, bang. "Open up! Open up!" It was Ginny. I climbed out of bed, staggered to the door, and opened it. Ginny stood there, wide eyed. "Larry! I had no idea how big this lake is. It's as big as an ocean. Look!" She grabbed me by the hand and yanked me across the hall to the huge picture window in her bedroom.

As a kid growing up in the house, I had experienced Lake Ontario as part of our property, just as I had the huge lawn, sloping down toward the shoreline. But now, as I saw it for the first time in many years while holding hands with Ginny, I could understand her amazement. "My Lord, you grew up with this huge lake as part of your life! I could never have imagined such a thing, growing up in the flat, dry prairies of Kansas. Listen to the noise of the waves! They put me to sleep last night. But I couldn't see them. Larry, what a wonderful place to grow up." She squeezed my hand more tightly, and then, to my surprise, lifted it to her lips and kissed it.

CHAPTER
16

That afternoon, almost all of my family came from near and far to my parents' reception for Ginny. Perhaps, as a good omen, the sky was bright blue, the slow, rolling waves luminous, and my mom and dad's huge, near one-acre lawn was festooned with decorations, including, to my great surprise, the flags of New York *and* the state of Kansas.

I think Ginny was overwhelmed by the sincere warmth of the welcome the family gave her. When Uncle Alan and Aunt Sonia arrived, she walked up to them and hugged each of them tightly. Sonia said, yet again, "You are such a lovely young woman. I enjoyed the fun we had at Ak-Sar-Ben, and I am so glad you've come to meet this rogue's gallery of Larry's family." The two hugged again, and Ginny walked back and joined the reception line, sliding her arm through mine.

In a couple of minutes, I could hear in the distance the throaty roar of what I knew was one of Uncle Rufus's sports cars. Rufus had various General Motors sales franchises—Chevy, Buick, Cadillac, and GMC trucks—all around Western New York. On this occasion, he thundered up to the party in a white Corvette with Holley Muffler and red leather interior. He arrived with a yes-I-am-here-so-the-party-can-start-now roar. After coming to a squealing halt on the over-sized, custom tires, he got out of his car, circled around, and headed toward the reception line without opening the door for his wife Rhona. This was typical of Rufus. After a brief pause, Rhona opened the door herself and followed him.

When Rufus got to Ginny, in his oily, car salesman way, he took hold of her hand with both of his, and held it so she couldn't escape, as if he was locking the door to one of his car showrooms until the prospective customer had finally been cowed into buying a car on his easy-payment plan at his extortionate, and in many cases illegal, interest rates. Still with Ginny's hand in his, he said, "What a lovely lady you are. Larry, as usual, has failed to tell us of your true beauty." I could see Ginny trying to pull her hand back to no avail. "But I," he continued, "do appreciate such beauty, in ladies such as yourself and in automobiles, such as that beautiful Corvette over there." He started to draw her hand to his lips to kiss it. With one sharp, very aggressive yank, Ginny pulled her hand from his, but he continued, "Virginia, have you ever driven a high-powered sports car?"

What could Ginny say?

Rufus continued. "I thought so! How about later in the day, I take you for a spin in that gorgeous car? Would you like that?"

Ginny, no wallflower, riposted "Sir, I don't really like the color of the car. It's much too small, it makes too much noise, and I suspect it needs a new muffler, which its owner was surely too cheap to install."

Chapter 16

I could barely suppress an outright laugh when it was clear that Rufus could not think of anything more to say and walked on.

Looking back at it, I see that reception as one of the kindest, most loving things that my parents had ever done for me, because apart from Rufus, my mom and dad, my uncles and aunts, and my cousins were all good people—honest, caring, straightforward, and hard working. And by the time that wonderful gathering came to an end, Ginny had not only enjoyed a true, loving embrace from my family but had come to feel the same for them.

Uncle Rufus, however, was not content until what he viewed as a loose end had been tied off. So, at his most oleaginous, he walked up to Ginny and held up the key to the Corvette. "Clearly, I failed to greet you appropriately and to express the warmth I truly feel. Please let me make amends by allowing me take you out in my sports car. I will teach you how to drive it with all the skills that a race car driver would use to travel safely on the street—how to shift by looking at the tachometer not the speedometer, how to downshift and double clutch, how to thunder from zero to sixty in under six seconds—in other words, how to handle the power of this top-of-the-line machine."

Ginny paused, then said, "Thank you, Mr. Pace, for that needed apology. So now, I would be happy to accept your invitation!"

Rufus of course ignored everything she had said except her last acquiescences to his wishes. They walked to the car, and I followed at a distance. Then, to my surprise, I saw Rufus climb into the passenger seat and invite Ginny to drive. I feel quite sure that Ginny saw this invitation for what it was: just another jab in the sparring match that she and Rufus had been engaged in. So whatever misgivings she may have had, she did not hesitate to climb into the driver's seat. Rufus told her how to start the car using the standard, five-speed shift and how to press the clutch before shifting. He then handed her the keys and said, "Start her up, my dear," knowing, I am sure, how offended Ginny would be by his calling her "dear."

Ginny got the car going and drove down Edgemere Road slowly. She initially ground the gears, but as the car disappeared into the housing development across the road, I could see that she was doing quite well and impressing upon Rufus what most of us already knew about Ginny the Librarian—that she is the quickest of quick studies.

About twenty minutes later, Ginny returned and brought the car to a sharp, high-speed stop that must have laid fifteen feet of rubber on the road and off Rufus' tires. She turned off the key peremptorily, handed it to Rufus, and said, "It seems to me that flashy show cars like this aren't really worth what I am sure people like you charge for them. I'll stick to my VW bus. But thank you." And without saying another word, she left the car, walked behind it, paused briefly to admire the two black streaks of rubber she'd laid, and returned to the party.

.

CHAPTER
17

The next day, Ginny and I joined my mom and dad at the local Presbyterian Church. The church was too small for the large congregation, so parishioners were stuffed into it as if into a sardine can. Year after year, the church trustees had presented to the members very expensive plans to enlarge the building, but these proposals were routinely denied. Instead, the parishioners approved a far less expensive addition inside the church: a second-floor balcony at the back with extra seating. To brighten the church, they added two dormer windows on each side. This allowed for the installation of stained glass windows that stretched from the dormers down the sides of the church to the height of the pews. The end result was a marvelous, intimate worship space, filled with sunlight and vivid, sparkling colors.

Aunt Sonia and Uncle Alan had met us at the church, and after the service, Aunt Sonia approached Ginny, and took her hand. "Remember at Ak-Sar-Ben when we had such a great time, we talked about rummage sales?"

Ginny replied, "I had forgotten! Can we do that now?"

"Of course!" Aunt Sonia said. She turned to me. "Larry, I'm not sure when your lovely girlfriend and I will be back, but don't worry. I'll drop her off at your parents' house with what I'm sure will be a large supply of beautiful dresses. Let's go, Ginny."

As I watched the two women leave, I felt a new burst of love for Ginny. She had agreed with some trepidation to leave Kansas to visit my family in New York, a foreign country to her. She had accepted my family's warmth and affection, and had jumped at Aunt Sonia's offer to go rummaging with her. I sighed deeply. And I knew then that I was at last ready to move on from Dell and that I would marry Ginny if she would have me.

Late in the afternoon, Aunt Sonia finally brought Ginny back to my parents' house. She came in with a glow on her face, no doubt reflecting the great fun she'd had with her new pal, Aunt Sonia, during their three-hour odyssey of drives to all of the churches with rummage sales in our area.

My parents invited Uncle Rufus and Aunt Rhona to join us for breakfast on Monday. At 8:00 sharp that day, they thundered into the driveway in a new, cobalt blue Chevrolet Corvette, with deep red leather seats. It was loaded with every possible option.

When we all sat down at the breakfast table in the little alcove off my parents' kitchen, we could see the shimmering beauty of the lake as the sun rose higher in the sky. After we finished breakfast, Rufus pulled out a large roadmap and carefully unfolded it on the table.

"This is a map of the state of New York," he said to Ginny, "which I wanted you to see so you would understand something. Many people hear 'New York' and think only of the big city down south, but if you look at the map you will see that New York is vast and pretty much underpopulated in the rest of the state, particularly in the western part where we are now.

"This area has an amazing and fascinating history, going back to the French and Indian War in the 1750s and 1760s. And it has more access to fresh water than any other state in the union—Lake Erie on the west; Lake Ontario on the north; Lake Champlain on the northeast (we share that one with Vermont and the Canadian province of Quebec); and the Hudson River, which flows due south from the Adirondack Mountains and is the only major river in the country that remains undammed. In the spring, the run-off from the melting winter snow in the Adirondacks turns the Hudson into a vast, boiling, dangerous cauldron of white water, threatening to leap its banks and blast all the way to the Atlantic Ocean, roaring past the US military academy at West Point, on the western side of the river.

"And then, of course, in this western part of New York, there are the eleven Finger Lakes—Conesus, Hemlock, Canadice, Honeoye, Canandaigua, Keuka, Seneca, Cayuga, Skaneateles, Otisco, Owasco—and innumerable small rivers. All this makes this part of the state lying west of the Catskills, south of the Thruway to the Pennsylvania border, and all the way to Lake Erie, one of the most productive farming areas in the world. We produce everything from wheat and fruit to high quality wines.

"You may have heard of the Erie Canal, which Governor DeWitt Clinton started in 1817. The canal ran east to west, essentially from Buffalo. At Rochester, it intersected with the Genesee River, which is one of the few in the world that runs north (the Nile River in Egypt being another).

"The canal was built so that all the produce from Western New York could be shipped east to the big cities. Its construction was complicated by the fact that the canal had to cross rivers in some places, so aqueducts were built to solve the problem. If you go into downtown Rochester, you can see that the bedrock of one of the city's major bridges is an Erie Canal aqueduct. You can still see the original gray rock of the aqueduct.

"I'm saying all this because I really want you, Ginny, to get to know this part of the state, which I love. So, if you want, you can have the brand new Corvette in the driveway for as long as you like. Drive it all over the state—five on the floor. I know you can handle the upshifting, downshifting, and huge disc brakes. My only concern is that I suspect you won't let Larry drive even once."

We all laughed, and I thought for just a moment Ginny's eyes moistened. She took both of his hands in hers and leaned a little toward him, so they were seeing eye to eye and said, "Rufus, thank you so much. I could not have imagined what you and the rest of your family would do for me in this visit. You are exactly right, I'm a farm girl from Kansas—kind of a flatland state. Like many Midwesterners, I and my family have a built-in feeling of inferiority in relation to all the people who live "back East." Being a flatlander from Kansas, I now realize that I never thought I would be treated with such warmth, generosity, and love, although," she said with a twinkle in her eye, "I did not anticipate that Larry and I would have a family feud over who would drive your beautiful car."

Ginny turned to me, fluttering her eyelashes, and said, "Larry, dearest. You won't have any objection if I drive the whole time, will you dear?"

I turned to Rufus and said with false sarcasm, "Thanks a lot, Uncle Rufus, for making me just a sightseer!" Everyone laughed, and then, after we finished our coffee Ginny headed toward the stairs and her bedroom to get her things.

Once she was out of sight and hearing, my mother came up to me, hugged me softly, and kissed me lightly on the cheek. She backed away a little so she could look me straight in my eyes.

"Dearest Lawrence. You are my only child," she said. "I birthed you, I changed your diapers, you cried on my shoulder, I helped you with your homework. I pretty much catered to your every whim, and all the while, every minute, I've loved you with an intensity that only mothers feel. And now, my heart is exploding with love for you and Ginny, so I'd like to give you this." She handed me a small box that held a wide, solid gold ring. The ring was made in a basket weave pattern and sparkled with tiny diamonds, rubies, and emeralds.

"This was your great-grandfather's engagement ring," my mother explained. "He gave it to Momma Katherine years ago. Great-Grandfather James had mined the gold himself during the great Alaskan gold rush of 1898. I'm so happy for you dearest, that you have found for yourself such a wonderful young woman. Please, take this ring with you. I have a suspicion it may come in handy in the near future."

CHAPTER
18

After hugs, kisses, and goodbyes, Ginny and I thundered off in Rufus' sleek Corvette, heading west along the lake shore to Niagara Falls. It sounds trite for married couples to go on their honeymoon there, but for some reason the falls have a romance that attracts honeymooners, so our going there was a sort of dry run—a should-we-be-honeymooners-or-not kind of trip. We crossed the Niagara River into Canada. Most people go there because the view of the falls is far better than it is from the New York side.

Ginny and I did the routine of signing up to go below the falls. We got our required rubber coats and hats so we could descend and be no more than ten feet from the water that was roaring past us. We were aware of the huge power lines that carry the electricity generated by the falls to Western New York.

Ginny was stupefied by the sight of the millions of gallons of water pouring over the falls. The memory of this spectacular place sticks with you till the end of your life. As we left, water still streaming down our raincoats, Ginny took my hand in her soft, firm grasp, lifted it to her lips and gave it a kiss. We left without talking and I got into the driver's side to drive us through the complicated route back to the U.S.

I got us across the river to a gas station, we filled up, and we switched places. Ginny took off, shifting, braking, and making tight turns, just as Uncle Rufus had taught her, clearly enjoying herself immensely. I think it was beginning to dawn on her that a ten-year-old VW bus was not the only option in life.

We drove to Chautauqua. Ginny greatly enjoyed its small-village charm, the beautiful lake, and especially the United Methodist House, which we visited. We then drove east along the New York-Pennsylvania border to Ithaca, where I took her to see Cornell University—particularly the law school. I explained my family's long history with Cornell. My Uncle Marvin and his wife, my Aunt Miriam, had both gone to Cornell—he from Rochester and she from Western New York near Forestville. They had met at the university, courted there, and then married after the end of the Great War. Ever since, they had been Cornell boosters, contributing money, attending reunions, and keeping in touch with events at the university.

I took Ginny through Hughes Hall, where the law school was located and where I had lived during my first year. I showed her the huge law library, which I think stunned her. She had never been to a law library, and as we walked down the main aisle between the towering bookcases perpendicular to us on each side, Ginny sometimes paused to look at the books themselves, remarking on how heavy and cumbersome they were.

Chapter 18

From there, Ginny and I walked to Cornell's world-renowned agricultural school, which, oddly enough, did not interest her. *So,* I thought to myself, *the woman loves books, not farming.*

Moving on, I showed her the Student Union. Outraged Black students had stormed and occupied the building to protest racism at Cornell and in the U.S. as part of the burgeoning Black Power Movement. Governor Rockefeller had sent in the National Guard to reclaim the Union.

Returning to Rufus' car, we drove to the Statler School of Hotel Administration, still on campus. I had reserved two rooms. After we each took some time to rest, we rode the elevator to the beautifully appointed dining room, where student wait staff served us a five-course gourmet meal prepared by other students who were on their way to becoming professional chefs.

Ginny loved the meal—the formality, the attention we received, but, most of all, the superb food. I explained that this gourmet restaurant existed as a treasure, almost unknown to the rest of Cornell's students. A guy could impress the lady of his eye with a superb meal for almost nothing.

After dinner, we retired to our rooms. I slept fitfully, and early in the morning, I got up, fixed some coffee, and walked onto my balcony, where I watched the bright sun slowly rise, illuminating the choppy blue waters of Cayuga Lake. As I looked out, my heart and mind took me back to my law school years.

CHAPTER
19

At Cornell, first-year students were required to live in Hughes Hall, where we slept, ate, and studied. We attended classes in contracts, constitutional law, administrative law, trusts and estates, and legal writing in Myron Taylor Hall. It was almost impossible for us to complete each day's assignments without staying up all night.

There were only two women in my class of one hundred twenty students. One was a short, quite pretty woman named Magda Bolduc, who was always cheery and humorous. The other was Lauren O'Neill, a blindingly gorgeous blond. She always wore obviously expensive clothing.

The problem was that with only two women in our class, we men had a hard time finding dates for the weekend. We quickly realized that we would have to look outside the law school. There were many undergraduate and graduate women on the Cornell campus, and there was always Wells College in Aurora, on the east side of Cayuga Lake. But our work at the law school was overwhelming, and classes were held from Monday through Saturday noon, so there wasn't much time for a search.

Still, I was determined, and I tried to approach Magda and Lauren. On one occasion, as I was climbing the staircase up to the landing between the second and third floor, I noticed Lauren ahead of me. She spotted me looking at her and said contemptuously, "So, is that the best you can get, Larry? Looking up a woman's dress?"

I replied, "Oh, no, I wasn't looking up your dress. I was puzzled by the lack of color coordination: the turquoise dress, your pink tights, the clunky shoes. I wondered, *What kind of a woman would dress like that?*" She paused, giving me just a flicker of a look that was a mixture of disdain and sadness.

The hardest day of the week was Saturday morning because we had mountains of assignments given to us on Friday, the day that had always been party time for most of us. To my credit, I kept studying after the end of Friday classes until I finished everything, wanting to make sure I was prepared if the professor called on me in class the next day.

I was particularly concerned about Professor Obermeir, who taught Contracts. One Saturday, the entire class was assembled when the professor swaggered to the lectern. He had before him a seating chart, since each of us was assigned to a particular seat. As Obermeir reached the lectern and looked down at his chart, we could see his finger move back and forth until it descended upon the name of a particular student.

"Mr. Pace," he called out. "Recite *Hagel v. Northwestern Railroad, Inc.*" I was ready. First, I briefly described the nature of the case, the question before the court, the law the court relied on, and the result the court reached. But Obermeir moved from behind the lectern and took two steps toward me. "Mr. Pace, you think that's good enough? Let's vary the facts a little bit."

So, as I anticipated he would, he began changing the facts, asking more questions as he did. In each case, I knew as well as he did, that there were no correct answers—just sensible responses to the pattern of facts he described. Shaking his fist and pointing his finger, he challenged me to justify each point of my responses, until finally, after standing for fifteen minutes, I got tired. When he varied the facts one more time, I could not think of a reasonable answer, and I made a fatal error, which, in the law game usually resulted in capital punishment.

"Professor," I said, "I don't see the point of that fact pattern. I have no response."

Obermeir took two more aggressive strides toward me, focusing his eyes only on mine. He spoke with virulent contempt. "Mr. Pace. Let me set the stage for you. You are a newly licensed lawyer, your wife is pregnant with your first child, you can barely afford the rent for your apartment, you are behind on your electric bill, and a client comes into your office, and puts $5,000 in cash on your desk and says, 'Get me out of this contract!' And you say, 'No, I can't help you?!'"

With his voice rising to a crescendo, he thundered, "You tell him YOU CAN'T HELP HIM?!"

I could feel the perspiration on my forehead and my knees beginning to weaken, but Obemeir did not let up. Almost shouting at me, he said, "Mr. Pace! The response to the question is in the footnotes, Mr. Pace. We all now know that you don't READ the footnotes. What good are you if you don't read the whole case? Including the footnotes!"

I sank back into my chair and Obermeir turned to the whole class. "I have graded all of the written snap quizzes that I gave you last week and the results were abysmal. Let me make this clear as a bell: you are here to study law so that you can be licensed by the state to practice law. The practice of law is just that—learning every day to be a better lawyer. Make no mistake about it, as lawyers you keep our society out of the lawless jungle. Instead of disputes being decided barbarically, they are decided by a legal system that seeks fair and just results, even though it often fails. All of you need to be clear that I will not tolerate the low level of scholarship that you are displaying and will see to a rapid early exit from this school by any one of you who doesn't measure up. Class dismissed."

I was so stunned by Obermeir's merciless attack on me, so embarrassed, that the next thing I remembered, I was somehow seated in the cafeteria at a two-person table. I had no recollection of having walked out the class door and down the hall to the lunchroom.

As I sat numbly at the table, Magda slipped into the chair opposite me. Patting me on the hand, she said, "Larry, don't take that guy too seriously."

"How can I not take him seriously? He could give me a flunking grade and I'd have to be out of here. What terrifies me most is that I think his attack was personal. I'm not sure, but I think I've never heard him speak to other students the way he scalded me, including his attack on poor Rick Betts. He reduced Rick to tears."

I thought about how Obermeir invited students to his home for dinner with him and his wife. He never invited me. I was hurt, but I was at the bottom of the class. I felt awful. I knew I was somehow missing the boat.

"No, no, Larry," she said. "You don't get it. My father is a businessman and a lawyer. He told me that the law game is brutal. You have to be tough to succeed. Obermeir was testing you. He wanted to see how you would fight back if he challenged you the way practicing lawyers are regularly challenged." She took my hands in hers and continued, "You passed. You had an answer for each of his questions to you. I could tell when you spoke that your responses were proper because you knew that there were no right or wrong answers to his questions. There are only considered responses based on the facts, and you banged the ball back to him again and again. My guess is that you really pissed him off when, after all of that good work, you looked like you were caving in the end. You had a point. You can alter the fact patterns until the end of the year and there would be no one answer. But he was demanding that you keep going and he's the one calling the shots."

When she finished, I squeezed her hand and said, "Thank you, Magda, you've been kind and realistic. I appreciate it very much. I won't let that son of a bitch steam roll me again."

"Good!" she said. That's the kind of guy I know you are. So, I have an idea. You're a handsome guy, I'm a gorgeous woman, how about a shack up every Saturday after lunch? We can get a hotel room, spend the afternoon and night, and then come back to school on Sunday morning. I know I am not ever going to make it through this pressure cooker without lots of good old sex. Do you think you can handle that?"

I looked straight into her eyes, saw that she meant it, stuck out my hand, and said "Deal. Let's shake on it."

CHAPTER

20

Magda's and my agreement did wonders for my morale. Whenever I felt lost in legal studies during the week, I knew the weekend with her would make everything better.

As we sat in classes, we all took notes, some a page or two and others several pages. I noticed that Lauren O'Neill kept notes only on three by five index cards. When it was her turn to recite cases, she stood straight, looking gorgeous, and spoke solely to the core questions posed and answered in the case. I took copious notes. But in the end, I realized that the importance of a case can be reduced to its core. Ultimately, that's what judges are looking for—not reams of paper but the point.

The hard work continued, day after day. In fact, to me, the volume of cases to be read and other class preparations were more than I and many others could handle. It was obvious, though, that there was method in the professors' meanness: they were separating the wheat from the chaff. I could sense who in my large class would not be around for the second year.

The school year finally ended and those who were culled began to make themselves known. One guy offered a complete set of books covering the subjects we'd read over the year. They were still in the packing case with a handwritten note on top: "These books are for the taking." Signed: "A wiser one."

I was tired of the law, the constant confrontations, and the anxiety they produced in me, so, unlike most of my classmates, I chose not to look for a summer internship in a law firm. I wanted to bail from the law completely for a few months, though I intended to return in the fall.

Since Cornell had notified us that they would not provide housing to second-year students, Magda and I decided to look for a place together. The key was to find a place as close to campus as possible, given that neither of us had a car. Because the housing market was highly competitive, we decided to find an apartment and sign a lease immediately, hoping to avoid the crunch in the fall.

The first apartment we found was at the end of College Street, giving us the easiest possible walk to campus. We knocked on the door of the landlord, a Mr. Culver, and a gruff, unshaven man answered, chewing tobacco as he spoke. He was a hard ass. "If you wants dis apartment, you gotta put down a deposit and first month's rent now. No checks. I've learned you spoiled brats at this big-time college are a bunch of crooks. No bouncing checks for the deposit or the rent when it comes due. Always all cash! Got it?"

Magda and I looked at each other, trying to discern if the other had access to the needed cash. I turned to the landlord and snapped, "How do you want it? Fives? Tens? Twenties? Fifties?"

"Whatever," he said. "So long as it adds up."

Magda turned to the man. "I'm sure you understand that's a lot in cash. I have an account at Ithaca Trust down in the city. It'll take me at least forty-five minutes to get down there, get the cash, and come back."

"Yeah. But if somebody comes by who's already got the money, you don't get the place. Got it?"

At that point, I snatched the key from his hand and said, "Look pal, we're getting this apartment. We're law students. If you mess with us, we will tie you up in court with huge legal bills. In a heart beat we'll do it. So you can wait here, or you can wait in our apartment."

I saw a flicker of boiling rage in his eyes, but the landlord took a deep breath. "Fuck the two of youse! I ain't afraid of nothin'." He paused briefly. "I'm going to get the fucking lease."

As he started toward the stairs, I reminded him, "Don't forget we need two copies. One for you and one for us."

"You fucking lawyers," he muttered, but he turned to go. A few minutes later, he returned with the leases. I made sure they were exactly the same. I started to sign one, but the guy said, "No signing until the cash is here. Then we sign. Got it?"

Magda left for the bank, and while we waited for her to return, I thought I'd try to talk with the man. "Mr. Culver," I said, "It's pretty clear to me that you know what you're doing with these rentals. How many have you got?"

Glaring, he replied, "I got lots of them. And they're filled with spoiled snots just like you."

"Now look, Mr. Culver, I don't want to get off on the wrong foot with you. I know how hard it is to be a landlord. You're nice to the tenants, you take care of them, and then they leave without paying the last month's rent. Or they wreck the place and then leave."

He sighed. "Yeah. Dat's right. Thing is, it's tough. And all that legal stuff—building codes, town requirements, the university. It's hard. I get taken advantage of, over and over. It's because of you lawyers. You're so expensive, I can't hire you. No offense, but I gotta protect myself."

"Of course you do, but I absolutely guarantee you won't have problems with me and Magda. If we don't see eye to eye on something, we'll invite you in for coffee and we'll talk it through. We will treat you as well as you are entitled to be treated. That is a promise." I put out my hand.

Culver took it in his huge, rough hand, and for a moment I thought he might take the opportunity to crush my hand with his python-like squeeze. He didn't, and with that one gesture, we made a kind of peace.

Right on cue, Magda arrived with the money. She and I signed both copies of the lease, paid what we owed, and unlocked the door to look at the apartment we had rented, sight unseen.

It was a nice place! There had been a screened-in porch in the front that had been closed in and weatherized. Beyond it, we saw a living room with a sofa, a Barcalounger, and an easy chair. A dining room table stood in front of a tiny kitchen. A small bedroom was reachable through a door just beyond the living room chair, and, in an odd twist, the shower and toilet were only accessible through a door in the bedroom—go figure. But I was impressed by the quality of Mr. Culver's work. The porch was air tight. All the walls in the apartment had been recently painted a pale off-white. The floors had been sanded and stained, and the window behind the couch had been thoroughly winterized.

When we saw the bedroom, Magda and I looked at each other. It contained only a twin bed. We each tried it out. Then, to our surprise, Mr. Culver arrived, carrying the parts of a big double bed, which he even put together for us.

CHAPTER
21

Madga and I parted ways, and I headed to New York City for a summer job I'd found through my best friend, Steve Parr, who was leaving Cornell. When I'd told him I was sick of the law and didn't want to have anything to do with it until the fall, he mentioned that his stepfather, Lorris Johnson, had a job that would be right up my alley.

Mr. Johnson had created a corporation in New York City called Heavy Water Holdings. He'd invented a process for making heavy water—a product used for cooling atomic power plants. With architects, he'd designed a factory for making this unusual substance. The firm's offices were closed for the first eight weeks of summer, and my job was to organize hundreds of rolled up architectural drawings so that all of the plans for each section of the factory would be together. As it was, they were strewn throughout the entire office.

Mr. Johnson met me at the office to make sure I understood the task at hand. When he was satisfied that I knew what I was doing, he handed me the keys, saying with a smile, "You may use these keys any time. Let yourself in here—midnight, daybreak, sunset, whatever. Make your own hours. I'll pay you $1,500 when the job is done." My dream job! Something that took me light years away from anything connected to the law.

Steve gave me the name of a good friend of his, Jim Oxenschlagger, who had an apartment I could share. Oxenschlagger and I agreed on my share of the rent. He went to his job in the morning and came home in the evening, but for me, time stood still. On a typical day, I worked at the office from the early morning until noon, when I had lunch at a great deli. At two o'clock I caught a matinee.

After the movie, I strolled back to the apartment, where Oxenschlagger and I had supper. Early on in my stay, at the end of one of our meals, Jim said, "Now it's time for dessert." He drew from his pocket what looked like a large fire cracker with a black fuse. It was filled with pot.

I begged off. I had tried some pot previously and it had done nothing for me. Besides, I had clearly in my mind my father's example. He'd quit smoking cold turkey when he was in his mid-forties because he'd sensed that smoking was horrible for the lungs. As a result, I had never smoked cigarettes or a pipe. The only exception was one time at summer camp, when I decided to smoke a cheroot—a small cigar. I had hoped to impress a girl at the camp, but she wouldn't have anything to do with a guy who smoked dirty little cigars trying to look like Clint Eastwood in a spaghetti western. I should have followed my father's example.

In late July, I got a call from my mother who told me that a letter had come from Cornell, addressed to me. Because of its probably importance, I asked her to read it to me over the phone.

"Dear Mr. Pace," she read. "Due to your low academic standing, you will not be permitted to return to Cornell without first appearing before a panel to show cause for our allowing your return. The panel will convene on July 31 at the law school. If you are not able to attend at that time, please call the registrar at 1-607-255-4232 to schedule another time convenient for all concerned."

"Sweetheart," my mother said, "you need to be there in a few days. Can you do that?"

I took a deep breath. "Yes, I can. Don't worry, Mom. I will be there and everything will work out ok."

"I know it will, sweetheart."

Despite my cheerful tone, I prepared to leave for Ithaca with some trepidation.

CHAPTER
22

The Cornell panel consisted of Drew McCane, the dean of admissions; Professor David Curtis; Professor Obermeir; and Dr. Eric Foulk, who was the school librarian.

I dressed formally for the meeting in a blue blazer and tie, steeling myself for a hard and embarrassing inquisition. Once the meeting was called to order and the panelists began to question me, it became clear that they were encouraging me. Oddly enough, Obermeir wanted me to return.

"Mr. Pace," he said, "I note from your transcript that you failed to pass the first year largely because of poor performances on written tests. That happens sometimes. There are students who are not good at test taking, though they may be otherwise talented. I was impressed by your performance in my Contracts class. You were prepared and did extremely well when I called on you. Your mind is nimble. I would hate to see you leave us."

Professor Curtis agreed. "I share Professor Obermeir's positive assessment and hope that you will return. I can attest to how well you conducted yourself."

"What can we do to help you do better in your second year? How about if we assign you a mentor to help with whatever you might be finding hard?" Professor Obermeir asked.

Professor Curtis jumped in. "I think that's a marvelous idea. I would be happy to serve as a mentor to Mr. Pace. But how about if we call this an assignment of a 'faculty advisor?'"

For just a split second, I thought I was going to cry. I had expected the committee members to be perfunctory inquisitors, but they had instead told me that they were invested in my making the grade. "Professor Curtis, I would appreciate it very much if you would be my faculty advisor," I said. "I certainly accept your offer."

Dean McCane called the meeting to an end. "Thank you all for coming. Mr. Pace, I wish you the best in the coming year. Don't be afraid to seek help from Professor Curtis or anyone else. Remember, we let you in and we have a vested interest in your succeeding. You are not alone. We will be talking with several other students before the term begins."

I shook hands with the panelists and left, feeling almost as if I were floating on air. The trip back to New York passed in a flash, as did the next few days. I finished my work for Mr. Johnson, collected the $1,500 check, and headed to LaGuardia, looking forward to spending a few days in Rochester with my family.

CHAPTER
23

I'd tried to reach Magda all summer, leaving many messages, but she never responded. Though I kept thinking she'd call me, she never did. I tried again when I was in Rochester, and then finally I gave up. Since she was from New Jersey, I tried to hire a New jersey detective to look for her.

As I started to tell him what I wanted, the detective stopped me. "Look. I can't take your money, buddy. Everybody around here knows what happened. There were two factions in Magda Bolduk's family, and there was a shooting. When it was all over, Magda and the rest of her family were dead." After a brief pause, he added, "I'm real sorry for your loss, but you should know that the two factions were fighting for control of a major crime syndicate that ran the docks in Bayonne. Your girl's family came out on the short end. A very short end."

I was stunned and horrified by the thought of Magda's being gunned down in a mob turf war. I couldn't stop thinking of her small body, bleeding on the street. My parents comforted me as I put my head into my hands and wept.

It was so good to be home, but I had to go back to Cornell after just a few days rest. As we talked about my departure, I thought aloud about my housing and then asked, "Can I give you the $1,500 I earned this summer for your old Dodge Dart?" My parents immediately said no. "Just take the car," they said, so I loaded in my things and drove back to Cornell.

I had $1,500 cash and a new bank account, but my immediate problem was to find a roommate. There was no way I could afford to cover the entire rent that I had planned on splitting with Magda. I put flyers around the law school to let people know I was looking for a roomie, but most had already finalized their plans for housing. Only a couple of guys were interested, and I didn't like either of them.

On the day that classes started, I was standing at my locker when Lauren McIntyre approached me. She was sun tanned and wearing a beautiful dress, her golden hair carefully coiffed and falling on her shoulders. The sweet scent of very expensive perfume preceded her.

We greeted each other and talked briefly about what we'd done during the summer, but as I would soon learn, Lauren like to get quickly to the point. "Larry," she asked, "have you found a roommate?"

"No, I haven't. I guess everybody's already made their plans."

"Well, I'm in a bit of a pickle. I had a place lined up but it just fell through. So here," she said, stretching out her arms, "is your roommate from heaven."

I was speechless. How could I not want a roomie as gorgeous as Lauren? It also quickly occurred to me, that she, as an in-house, first-in-the-class, law review editor might make it easier for me to get my schoolwork done.

So I said, "Lauren, this would be great for me, too. Just so you know, the rent is $750 a month, split between us."

I started to describe the place, particularly it's best feature, which was the short walk between the apartment and campus. She stopped me midway. "Let's go take a look."

We walked to the apartment, which Lauren liked immediately, especially the weatherized porch. She viewed it as a perfect bedroom and study. She let it be known that she didn't need a double, so the twin bed went into her room. The landlord put in a long desk that she divided into two sections—one for classwork and one for the law review.

It took us a couple of weeks to work out a routine. I tended to get up early, reviewing my notes while eating a simple breakfast at the small table. I'd leave a breakfast for Lauren before I bolted to the law school, where I'd spend more time preparing for the day's classes. Lauren tended to stay home until her first class or whatever appointment she might have had. She usually needed many hours for going through the materials for classes and the law review.

I envied Lauren's study technique. She'd scan a page for ten seconds or so and then move on to the next page, by which time the materials were locked in her brain. As I observed her, I was astounded by her ability to finish everything as quickly as she did. I had never before met anyone with her level of brain power.

Lauren and I tended to return home from campus at different times. She came back relatively early, no later than nine o'clock, so she could get a good night's sleep. I usually ground away at my carrel until at least ten o'clock, if not later. I was very careful to unlock the apartment door and prepare for bed as quietly as I could.

The fact that the shower and toilet could only be reached through my bedroom made things complicated, however. At night, if Lauren wanted to use the bathroom, she had to get up from her front porch bed and walk across the living room into my bedroom. She would shut the door to use the toilet, then tip toe across the room to get back to her bed.

I'm pretty sure that each of us felt, if only subconsciously, the inevitability of our becoming lovers. Overworked, exhausted law students didn't have time to look around for companionship outside the law school.

One night, after she'd finished in the bathroom, Lauren slipped into my double bed, pulled up the covers, and fell sound asleep. I didn't know she was in bed with me until I woke up in the morning, but from then on, we spent every night together.

When we did finally approach lovemaking, we were passionate and free wheeling—free wheeling because, even though I offered to put on a condom, she would not let me enter her.

"You can do anything else you want. But not that. I don't care if you have a condom. I cannot risk getting pregnant. I will not let myself get pregnant."

I could hear the fear in Lauren's voice. "Well, that's fine," I said. "Whatever you are comfortable with is fine, Lauren." I hugged her and kissed her. We put our arms around each other and fell sound asleep.

In the middle of the night, one time, I heard yelling and

screaming. I woke up to find Lauren next to me, asleep, but shouting and crying, "No! No!" She got quiet again and never did wake up from her dream.

The next morning, a Sunday, I woke up as usual and made coffee. Lauren woke up ten or fifteen minutes later. She propped herself up on pillows. I handed her a cup of coffee then got into bed next her. After we each got our necessary caffeine hit, I turned to her and said, "Sweet heart, why don't you tell me what happened?"

She paused, looked at me, and answered, "Fair enough."

CHAPTER
24

Lauren took a deep breath and then started.

"I grew up in a very rich suburb of St. Louis called Clayton. My father graduated from MIT summa cum laude with a degree in aeronautical engineering. He chose the St. Louis area because McDonnell Aircraft, which was based there, made him the best offer.

"The U.S. Navy was McDonnell's only customer, and my father worked on Navy jets for years. He developed a classic design that was effective for some time. His genius was that he understood that the conversion of planes from piston engines to turbine power meant a huge increase in the amount of fuel that would be needed.

"My father saw that the key factor in any design would be how much fuel the fighter jet could carry. Fuel load determined the plane's combat range. He and several other engineers at McDonnell saw that the best place to put the fuel was in the fuselage, placing the two engines in small bubble fairings on the undersides of the plane. This increased fuel capacity greatly, in contrast to the planes offered by Grumman or Vought, who had opted to put the engines of their planes in the fuselage and who were therefore forced to place external fuel tanks on the wing tips.

"My father's designs prevailed, starting with the first Phantom; continuing with the F2H Banshees used in the Korean War; and finally, with the world-renowned Phantom II. I think the designs were even used in the F4U-1, though those were built by Vought.

"McDonnell built more than four thousand planes that were bought by numerous other countries. My father and his team were the ones who designed the Phantom's unique, horizontal tail wing, which folded down, while the wings' outer panels were angled upwards. These designs made the Phantom incredibly dangerous, feared by all opponents.

"As a kid, I really liked those times because many foreigners came to St. Louis to pick up their planes or participate in design conversations. My parents threw lots of parties for them, and I got to meet a range of people—Germans, Brits, Koreans, Japanese, and Israelis. I remember my dad liked the Brits best. They requested changes in the Phantom's design because they wanted to use their own engines—not the usual J79 GEs, but Spey turbo-fan jet engines, which greatly increased the range of the jets.

"My father did well and had a huge salary. This made my mother happy. She and Dad were a team. Their goal was to move Dad up the ladder, hopefully, to the presidency of the company. Mother held garden parties and socialized whenever she could with the wives of McDonnell executives, while my father devoted himself to his engineering work.

"We had an enormous house. Our family was moving up

in the world, and I did well in school. I had everything, but I felt that my parents cared most about Dad's achievements as an engineer and his climb up the ladder. My academic successes were just used for bragging rights.

"When I graduated from high school, cum laude, the question was where I'd go to college. Unbeknownst to my parents, I'd begun seeing my school's guidance counselor, John Harvey, initially to express my frustration with my parents. As he and I continued to talk, he eventually said, 'Lauren, you need to be clear. Your parents are abusing you— not physically or sexually, but emotionally. They are using you as a prop in their efforts to get your father to the top of McDonnell. They do not love you.'

"I surprised myself because I did not feel anguish over what Mr. Harvey told me. I felt elated—freed, like a beautiful balloon floating up toward the sky. 'You and I are going to make a plan so that you can get the heck out of here and never come back,' he said.

"We decided to turn my parents' selfish social climbing against them. We knew they would forbid me to go to any college in the East unless we sold my acceptance there as yet another wonderful achievement that would give them additional bragging rights. Co-ed schools were out of the question because they imagined a glorious, high-end wedding to a man from a prominent *local* family—more bragging rights for them.

"Our pitch to them was that I would go to one of the Seven Sister Colleges in the northeast—Smith, Holyoke, Wellesley, Radcliffe, Bryn Mawr, Vassar, or Barnard. I was accepted by all of them, but my parents only liked Bryn

Mawr. We'd described it to them as a Quaker college, and like many people in the Midwest, they saw Quakerism as a religion that forbade pre-marital sex."

CHAPTER
25

"Bryn Mawr was an eye-opening experience for me. My parents had overlooked the fact that Haverford, the nearby men's college, had a kind of sister-brother connection. Students from the two campuses commonly dated each other.

"I let loose. I went out with whomever I wanted and stayed out late. My girlfriends and I often joined the guys we liked at the Blue Flame Diner when we were returning to Bryn Mawr from Haverford. But then I met Tom Muthoni, an African student at Haverford who was a Quaker from Kenya. We were exact opposites. He was the blackest person I'd ever seen, unlike the African Americans I'd known at home. As stunned as I was by his appearance, he was equally stunned by mine—my white skin and long blond hair.

"The dating scene was a little chaotic. Students went out in groups—sometimes to Penn football games at Franklin Field, with its gorgeous brick stadium; now and then to see the Eagles or the Phillies play; and sometimes just to the movies. We'd become a pack that roamed the area looking for a good time during our brief time-outs from studying. Gradually, we split into pairs—straights and gays. Tom and I started sleeping together in his dorm room at Barclay Hall.

"At the end of the academic year, Tom went home to Kenya for the summer. I talked my way into a good job as a waitress at L'Isle de France, the best high-end restaurant in the area. By the end of the summer, I had raked in over $1,500. I was pleased, but by the time I left the restaurant, I knew that I was pregnant. I had missed my period and I had a little bump in my belly.

"I do not know how my parents learned of my condition. Somehow, they did, and they summoned me back to Missouri. I refused to go, but a few days later my father called me and said in the sternest voice he'd ever used, 'Lauren, you are coming back. You know that we do not believe in pre-marital sex or in legal or illegal abortions. Most of all, we will not have your horrible bad judgement stain our family. So which is it? Either I come and get you or you spend some of the money you earned to fly back here. If you are not back here within forty-eight hours, I will come and get you. You choose.'

"'I wouldn't want you to actually have to spend time and your own money to get me back there,' I said, 'but I'm telling you that I do have my own money, I know who I am, and I will be home in four days, not forty-eight hours.' Dripping with sarcasm and venom, I added, 'Take it or leave it.'

"After a long pause, my father snarled, 'If you're not back in four days, believe me, Lauren, you will pay the price. We will not let you sully your family's good reputation as Christians.'"

CHAPTER
26

"Four days later, my father picked me up at the St. Louis airport and drove me directly to a home for unwed mothers about sixty miles north of Clayton. He dropped me off and left without a word. I thought the place would be horrible, but I soon found that I was among kind and supportive people. That was true of the staff and of the fifteen women who were staying there until after they gave birth.

"When my time came, and I gave birth to a nearly eight-pound boy, the nurse gave him to me for just a moment. I saw Tom in the child. Then, without warning, the nurse quickly pulled him from me and I never saw him again. He was taken away for adoption.

"I think I became clinically depressed after my son's birth. I stayed at the home, never wanting to leave, as if my life had come to an end. Then, gradually, my bond deepened with the other women in our group sessions, where each of us could express our deep sense of loss.

"There was, however, one shattering difference between me and the other mothers: when it came time for them to leave, their families or loved ones picked them up and drove them away. I had experienced that kind of caring while I was in the home, but as I finally stepped out the door to leave, I realized that I was alone. My parents had not come to meet me.

"The director who ran the facility was not surprised. As I stood at the door alone, tears rolling down my face, she pulled up in a large car, told me to jump in, and handed me three thousand dollars in cash. 'I'm driving you directly to St. Louis International Airport,' she said, 'where you are to purchase a one-way ticket for anywhere you want to go back East. Never go back to your horrible, degrading parents. Cleanse them from your mind as best you can, and look forward. What will you make of your life now?'

"I flew back to Philadelphia and returned to Bryn Mawr on the Paoli local from the 30th Street Station. I'd missed an entire year, but I returned to do what I always did well: I excelled in my classes as an A student. With glowing recommendations and record-high LSAT scores, I applied to all the Ivy League law schools and was accepted everywhere.

"I called Mr. Harvey, my high school guidance counselor to ask his advice. He strongly recommended Cornell, frankly saying that Harvard and Yale were elitist schools. Cornell, though it was an Ivy League university, had a long history of opening its doors to all kinds of people. He thought I'd feel more comfortable here, and in any case, a Cornell law graduate would be pretty much able to write her own ticket after graduation.

"So that's how I ended up here at Cornell, Larry. And it's working out well. I'm first in my class, I'm the editor of the Law Review, and now I have a wonderful man for a lover."

Chapter 26

Pointing her finger at my chest, she said, "That would be you, Lawrence," and she gave me a hug.

CHAPTER
27

My second year went better and better as the months passed. Professor Curtis kindly reached out to me to remind me that he would always be available to help. I started taking Professor Hogan's classes on the Uniform Commercial Code. As it turned out, Professor Hogan and I developed a sympatico relationship because as I studied the Code, I began to share his interest in it and to understand why it is essential to the lives of everyone in our country.

In his lectures, Professor Hogan told us that before the enactment of the Code, commercial transactions not involving real estate were governed by a briar patch of laws that varied from state to state. The Code covered everything, from how to deposit a check, to how to make "secure transactions"—purchases bought on time and not covered by mortgages.

I was fascinated by the Code. Professor Hogan and I sometimes had lunch together so we could talk about one arcane point or another. I did well in his class, which gave me more confidence, and I began to enjoy my studies in ways I hadn't during the first year.

In my third year, although the course load was light, it featured two vital subjects: Advanced Document Drafting and Advanced Evidence. Professor Roberts taught the Evidence class, and rumor had it that there was always a big surprise at the end of the last class.

Sure enough, on the last day, the professor stood and announced, "Students, I've been so happy to teach you. I found you to be bright and inquisitive." Suddenly, we heard yelling and a man ran in, chasing someone else. In front of the entire class, after a struggle, he shot the man dead and ran out the door. We were aghast. Students were screaming.

Professor Roberts looked at his seating chart and called out, "George McGee, are you present today?"

A reluctant student raised his hand.

"Please tell me what you just saw," the professor demanded.

The student stood and said, "Well, a guy came running into the building, and then another guy came after him. They fought to the death and shot each other."

Professor Roberts looked at his seating chart again. "Mr. Smith, Mr. Paul Smith, you, way in the back, what did you see?"

His voice shaking, Paul said, "I saw a murder. A cold-blooded murder. In a law school!"

"Please tell me what you saw, sir, not what you saw at the end, but describe the entire string of events."

After he'd spoken, Professor Roberts continued, pointing out the contradictions between the two accounts. "The lesson is clear. In the study of evidence, eyewitness testimony is some of the most unreliable. In any case, when there is testimony by an eye witness, it should be viewed with a clear understanding of the inherent weakness of that person's perceptions, for they have inevitably been influenced by strong emotions. You therefore must always search for corroborating evidence.

After the dead man stood up and the two actors left the room, the professor continued.

"Let me give you an example, though, of how difficult it is to impugn an eyewitness's testimony. When I first got out of law school, I worked for a firm in Topeka that periodically did pro bono criminal defense. In this particular case, a night-time burglar was trying to steal jewelry from a bedroom bureau when the woman who was asleep there woke up. The woman later appeared in court as a prosecution witness and claimed that she had been able to see the burglar because of the night light above her bureau.

"As a defense attorney for the accused, I questioned the woman repeatedly about the brightness of the light, her distance from the burglar, and the darkness of the room, attempting to cast doubt on her identification. She asserted several times that she could recognize the man because she had seen him for at least nine seconds. When I sat down, the prosecutor stood up to cross examine. He did only one thing: he pointed to the clock on the wall and counted off nine seconds. Those nine seconds felt mighty long to me and everyone else.

"I was a new lawyer then, so there's more to the story. I stood again and basically accused the witness of ignorance of the implications of her testimony. 'I don't think you really understand the consequences of what you're saying—of this identification!'

"'Oh yes, I most certainly do,' she said. 'I would never make a serious allegation like this if I weren't certain. I understand exactly the consequences. My husband spent fifteen years in the Missouri state penitentiary.'

"So," Professor Roberts continued, "this story should answer the question I know you've all been asking. 'Why did Professor Roberts become a professor? Why didn't he practice law?' The answer is that no one would hire an attorney who would come out with such questions and comments. Thus, I am in a position to share my wisdom with you: Don't ever ask a witness a question if you don't already know the answer to it yourself!"

We students stood up, clapping and cheering, and that was the last class of our third year.

Chapter
28

Lauren and I spent the night before graduation in our apartment making love, talking, and coming to grips with the fact that very shortly each of us would go in different directions. Our love affair, which we treasured and which was so essential to keeping us both on track would come to an end.

After we settled final payment with Mr. Culver and got the deposit back, we were ready for graduation. My strong performance in the last two years of school had boosted my class rank up from the bottom. Many of my compatriots who had done very well in the first year had struggled in the second and third. But none of that mattered in the end.

The graduation ceremony was the most wonderful experience I'd ever had. The dean of the law school gave a short speech, urging us to do our best to make the public appreciate the value of lawyering. After he finished, he introduced Lauren as our valedictorian.

Lauren had worked hard to prepare and was ready to speak. She walked to the podium wearing her black gown and cap, her long golden hair gathered by a simple clip. She took the lectern and began her speech, which was succinct and, as always, blunt. First, she enjoined us to be good lawyers, but also to be great people. She urged us to engage in public service, continuing in that vein until the end, when she said, "Most of all, remember, you are people licensed by the state to make the rule of law work fairly throughout our society. Never forget that function and that nearly everyone you will ever meet will have something to show you, something to teach you. So always listen carefully to others. Always remember the people who helped you reach this moment—family, professors, and good friends, like the friend Larry Pace was to me. He taught me the values of loving and being loved. He got me through the long nights. Thank you, Larry, for all you did. And thanks to all of you. Go forth and be great!"

Lauren stepped back in the midst of sustained applause. The of the board of trustees read each of our names and each of us passed by the podium to receive our diplomas.

After the ceremony was completed and families gathered to congratulate the graduates, my family gathered around me, but Lauren was alone. I walked over to her, took her hand, and introduced her to my mother and father. They were warm and kind and deeply admiring of her.

At last, the crowd thinned. The parents and graduates disappeared. There was nothing left to do but begin the summer. Lauren and I said goodbye. She headed for New York City and I for Rochester.

CHAPTER
29

I sat for a long time on the balcony, remembering my law school years, but when I at last heard Ginny making herself a cup of coffee, I knew it was time us to leave. We loaded our luggage into the car and took our time driving, at first, enjoying East Shore Drive and lovely views of Lake Cayuga. Then Ginny took the wheel. By this time, she had thoroughly mastered the powerful car, shifting by watching the tachometer, per Rufus's instructions. In fifth gear, she was doing one hundred. I strongly reminded her that the speed limit was sixty-five and that she had only a five-mile grace above that. She obligingly throttled back to ninety, and it was at that speed, a few miles later, that she blasted through a state police radar trap. She immediately throttled way back, but it was too late.

Very shortly, blue lights were flashing behind us, and she had to pull to the side of the Thruway. As the officer approached the car, she said, "Larry, get the registration out of the glove box!"

I replied, "Are you out of you mind?! When an officer is

approaching a car like this, you must absolutely make sure he can see your hands."

Ginny glanced at me, looking puzzled, but my conceit was that, as a librarian, she loved me even more, because I had imparted to her a new fact. By then, the officer had arrived at our window. I told him that I would need to open the glove compartment to get the registration. He replied, "Proceed."

Ginny handed him the registration, which was in Rufus's name, and her Kansas license. He examined them carefully and took them back to his cruiser. When he returned and handed them back, I thought I saw a kindly look in his eye.

"Ma'am," he said, "you were going a ninety miles an hour in a sixty-five-mile-an-hour zone where we give everyone five-miles-an-hour leeway. Because of your clean driving record, I will not require you to drive with me into the town of Malone, where you would normally have to pay this ticket. Here is the ticket. I am canceling the fine, but I will send notice of your violation to the Kansas authorities.

"I do want to make something very clear to you, though. The hardest part of my job is arriving at horrible, multi-car, multi-fatality crash sites caused by people driving the way you were driving. I've seen people screaming in pain, yelling for the jaws of life, or burned to a crisp, their cars so twisted we can't get them out. We officers are human beings just like you, and believe me, it takes some time for us to recover emotionally from these horrible crashes—not only because of what we have seen and heard, but because of our rage at people like you, who drive without any thought of the consequences and wreck so many of the lives of others. Drive carefully and have a good day."

Chapter 29

The officer turned and walked back to his cruiser. Ginny sat quietly on the shoulder of the road for some time after he departed. I suspect that never in her life had she been scolded in such a way, nor had she ever felt so ashamed of herself. She turned to me and asked, "Larry, would you please drive?"

We changed places and I drove back to my parents', where we spent the night before flying back to Kansas City.

CHAPTER
30

When we got back to Kansas City, Ginny and I each had catching up to do at work. For the next couple of weeks, we had lunch every day at the library and one or two dinners out, but that was it.

About a week after work finally let up, I invited Ginny to take a day trip south along the Missouri-Kansas border to the beautiful Tallgrass Prairie Preserve. It is a stunning place, where the grassland has never been plowed under, and where, among the grasses bloom yellow, green, and blue wildflowers.

Ginny had been to the park before, on several occasions, but even so, the sight was stunning. We had a light lunch at a restaurant. She talked with some passion about how much she had enjoyed my family. "I feel like they are a part of me!" Even a slug like me got the sub-text, so as we headed back north and the sun was slowly descending in the west, I pulled off into a small picnic area. As the huge, yellow sun passed its last warm rays over us, I took her left hand in mine. I opened the box my mother had given me and took out the gleaming, gold ring.

I slid the ring gently over the tip of Ginny's precisely manicured finger. Looking her straight in the eyes. I said, "Virginia Wood, I have fallen deeply in love with you, and I want us to be together, as husband and wife, *and* mother and father of a large family for the rest of our lives. Please accept my humble and heartfelt proposal of marriage."

Tears were now rolling down Ginny's cheeks. She bowed her head for a moment, then looked up. "Of course, my dearest love. I want to be with you until the very end of our lives, and I assure you that I will be not only a mother, but the most devoted wife to you that I can possibly be."

I slowly slipped the magnificent ring down her finger and over her knuckle, and with the rays of the sun making the gold ring glow and the tiny gems in it sparkle, she reached forward. We put our arms around each other and kissed.

When we got home that evening, we went to Ginny's condo. We first called her parents to announce our engagement. That produced an uproar that we could have heard from Wichita—never mind the phone. Then we called my parents and got the same response.

When I hung up, we realized that we would have no control whatsoever over our wedding. As if to drive that point home, like a spike being pounded into a railroad tie, when I got to work the next day, Arleen came into the office. "Just to let you know," she said, "I have appointed me and Oscar as your sole wedding planners."

I goggled at her. "How did you know?"

After a very short pause, she gave me the look that I had seen many times in the past, which meant, "Don't you know yet that I know everything about all matters impacting your performance at this firm?"

"Do you really think Oscar and I would leave all the details involved with your wedding to some overpriced, incompetent wedding planner?" she asked. "We will handle everything."

As I stood before her speechless, her tough demeanor softened, and she looked at me with her large, dark eyes, now moistening just a bit. "Larry," she said, "after all the years we've worked together, you know that I have come to respect you, like you, and most of all, care about you. I know you feel the same for me."

I had to bite my lower lip to keep back the tears. Then I saw, in a blur, tear drops falling on my shoes. She reached into her pocket and gave me her handkerchief. I blew my nose several times, we hugged solidly, and as we parted, she said, "Lawrence, you are one of most decent people I have ever met. You can rely on Oscar and me to make your wedding and the reception go off without a hitch."

I looked at her, kissed her on the forehead, and said, "What else is new? You've been saving my ass for years!"

We both burst into loud laughter, and she turned and headed to her office. At the door, though, she looked back and said, "You understand, Larry, this will *not* interfere at all with my duties as your senior paralegal and my obligation to push your nose to the grindstone generating billable hours."

I responded, "I would not have it any other way!"

CHAPTER
31

When I think back on it, truth be told, everything did go off without a hitch, just as Arleen had promised. Guests from out of town had reservations for excellent lodging, and Oscar picked them up at the airport in one of the firm's Mercedes. Arleen had reserved a large function room at the Muehlebach Hotel for the families' pre-wedding dinner meet-and-greet. She and Ginny had a great time working out the menu. They chose the liquor, wines, and hors d'oeuvres; decided on the table settings; and planned the seating. Arleen suggested Baked Alaska for dessert. Being from Kansas, Ginny had never heard of it, but she grabbed the suggestion and ran with it.

I think the reality of our getting married did not fully sink in for either of us until the pre-wedding dinner on Friday evening, when our two families enjoyed an open bar manned by two bartenders pouring Dewars Scotch, Key Kentucky bourbon, and other top shelf whiskeys. After what seemed to me to be a rather over-extended period of imbibement, our guests finally drifted, some clearly unstable, toward twenty circular tables, beautifully arranged with white tablecloths, fine silver, and brightly colored napkins striped in yellow (for the state of New York) and red (for the state of Kansas). At each table, men wearing expensive suits and women in revealing cocktail dresses enjoyed the services of the impeccable waitstaff (each chosen by Arleen) who delivered caviar appetizers; a light lobster Newburg soup; chicken cordon bleu; grilled, wild rainbow trout; prime rib; a medley of fresh roasted vegetables; and, of course, Baked Alaska for dessert—all washed down with glasses of well-aged Rothschild Châteauneuf-du-Pape and Domaine de la Romanée-Conti Montrachet.

When everyone was seated, my father rose and raised his glass. "Ladies and gentlemen, my wife Mildred and I are so pleased to host this marvelous gathering that brings our two families together as one. We still remember with great warmth Virginia's visit to our home in Rochester, New York, where we were able to experience first-hand what a charming and decent lady she is. We could not be happier for her and our son Lawrence. We know they will have a long and loving marriage, which will be a sparkling jewel for both of our families—the union of two fine people who have fallen in love and now look forward with great joy to their marriage tomorrow. So, please stand with me and join me in a toast to Virginia and Lawrence."

My father turned to Ginny on his right and me on his left, and said, "May your marriage be long, loving, and faithful, and a joy to both of you, as long as you both shall live!"

Even before my father was done, people were raising their glasses and cheering.

CHAPTER
32

When the wedding planning had begun, I had mentioned to Arleen that I would be spending Friday night at my house. She gave me her "Arleen look," which generally meant: You are really one dumb dude!

"I've made reservations for you at the Muehlebach, where all the families will be staying. Ginny will be there too, but I am not telling you in which room, because you may not see her before the wedding." Then, with her marvelous twinkle in her eyes, she added, "On pain of my mistyping all your papers for a year!"

Hearing her, I was again flooded with deep love for her, she who had for years been my professional colleague, but who had also treated me with the deepest kindness. She'd brought me from being an emotional wreck when Dell abandoned me to the point where I'd become a dominant law partner strong enough to love Ginny and to enjoy the sincere warmth of her love for me.

Ginny and I had several conversations with the minister, as a couple and individually. He spoke about the meaning of marriage, commitment, and the vow that only death would part us. I was relieved that he was easygoing and broad minded, and I was surprised by how calming the conversations had been. At our final meeting, he explained, "I am just trying to slow down your heart rates so you will be alive for the wedding!"

On the day of our wedding, I got to the church a good half hour early to meet with the friends who were my six groomsmen. Their rented tuxedos fit them perfectly because Arleen had gone with each of them to the store where they were fitted. From time to time, I peeked into the vast sanctuary, with its stone pillars, vaulted ceiling, and four hundred fifty seats, which were rapidly filling.

As I had my last look into the sanctuary, the minister arrived. I introduced him to the groomsmen. He said to all of us, with a twinkle in his eyes, "I hope one of you has the ring!"

For one brief, heart-stopping moment, I could not remember where the ring was, but Gary Bond, an old Cornell classmate, carefully reached into his vest pocket and brought out the ring. The minister, again with a twinkle in his eyes, asked, "Are you sure the ring will fit her?"

"Oh yeah, I chose it, but Arleen ordered it," I said. "So it must be perfect."

After what seemed like an eternity, though in fact was only about twenty minutes, the wedding ceremony began. The church was jam packed. The minister had kindly maneuvered me to where I was supposed to stand near the altar. As a hush came over the packed crowd, the minister signaled and in the upper balcony in the back, four trumpeters rose and began to play a fanfare. The procession began with our young nieces, who scattered rose petals. They were followed by Ginny's mother, escorted by Eric Carter, my best friend from law school, and my parents. The bridesmaids came next, each on the arm of one of my groomsmen.

Then at last, I saw Ginny on her father's arm. Her gleaming, white silk wedding gown clung close to her upper body and hips, then spread below her to the floor, swaying gently as she began to walk. A vast train of shining silk followed her, held by two of her nephews.

As she started down the aisle, our eyes met, just for a moment, but long enough for me to feel my heart growing within me. It beat strongly, pumping the bounty of my love for her through every vein and artery of my body to the end of the last capillary, teaching me the complete meaning of joy in the fullness of love.

As she progressed, the flower girls peeled off to the side. Eric, always the perfect gentleman, seated Mrs. Wood on the front row aisle seat of the bride's side of the church. When Ginny finally arrived at the altar, the perfectly timed music ended. The crowd settled into the quiet, and the minister began to recite in his soft, but powerful voice our obligations to one another as husband and wife.

After a brief pause, he turned to Ginny and said, "Do you, Virginia Wood, hereby take this man, Lawrence Kelley Pace to be your lawful husband, to help him, to guide him, to care for him, and to cleave only to him for as long as you both shall live?" Ginny looked straight at me and said for all to hear, "I do!" He then turned to me and asked the same question. "I do!" I said, forcefully enough for even the trumpeters to hear.

"May we have the ring, please?" the minister asked.

Gary, looking solemn, fished the ring out of his vest pocket and handed it to me. I took Ginny's hand in mine and slid the golden orb over her finger. Ginny then took my hand in hers, and slowly, her eyes moistening and locked on mine, slipped my ring onto my finger.

The minister intoned as loudly as possible, sending the words echoing to the end of the vast church, "I now declare you, Lawrence Kelley Pace, and you, Virginia Wood, to be husband and wife. Larry, you may now kiss the bride."

We kissed softly, at length, until the minister, loudly coughing, reminded us that it was time for the processional. Ginny slipped her arm through mine, and we started back down the aisle, again to the sound of the trumpets, friends cheering and clapping, wishing us well along the way until we reached the heavy entrance doors. We stepped onto the terrace and stopped, where our photographers took several pictures. As they did, Ginny's bridesmaids gathered at the foot of the steps, each hoping for her bouquet. After the lucky one caught it, they parted into two lines and threw white confetti at us as we walked across the lawn to the huge tent her parents had rented for our reception.

CHAPTER
33

Ginny's father Russell may have been a penny pincher, but not regarding the wedding of the daughter he adored. As Ginny and I entered the vast space where the reception was to be held, we saw brightly colored lanterns glowing from the top edge of the tent and scattered from the ceiling. Elegant, straight-backed, gold chairs circled fifty-seven round tables, each covered with long white table cloths and set for eight (soup spoons; dinner spoons; salad and dinner forks; dinner, butter, and steak knives—all obviously real silver—with three crystal wine glasses and a champagne flute). In the center of each table were bouquets of purple, lavender, and pale blue orchids in silver vases. On the left, next to a large dance floor, I saw a dance band—trumpet, trombone, clarinetist, and keyboard player, plus, of course, two guitarists and a drummer.

Ginny and I came to a dead stop, amazed by the beauty, detail, effort, and sheer cost of what we saw. My groomsmen escorted women without partners to their tables, finding the rectangular cards and reading the raised gold letters that marked the place for each. Russell and Jaclyn had provided a long table for Ginny, me, my groomsmen, and Ginny's bridesmaids. Arranged along the two sides and back of the tent, charcoal grills were manned by chefs, each responsible for preparing Kansas City prime sirloin steaks, teriyaki chicken and, for vegetarians, a medley of roasted vegetables. Each table was served by one white-gloved waiter who remained at the beck and call of the guests throughout the evening.

As soon as everyone was seated, an army of sommeliers entered, each pushing a tiny cart filled with a variety of wines that they began to pour for the guests. Waiters took orders for the chefs. The scent of the cooking food wafted through the entire enclosure. As people began eating, the band started to play—soft tunes, at first, but by the end of the meal, the musicians were pounding out real rhythm and the guests, replete with great food and wine were heading to the dance floor for a little boogie woogie.

When all was said and done—the dinner completed and the huge wedding cake cut—Uncle Rufus stood up, tapped his drinking glass with his knife, and began to speak. "Ladies and gentlemen, I am Rufus Pace, Larry's uncle. I have had the grand pleasure of meeting Larry's bride at my family's place on Lake Ontario in Western New York, when she was kind enough to greet us, and to charm us with her sophistication and beauty. We all quickly learned what a fine young woman she is. BUT, I feel compelled to inform all of you, particularly Ginny's parents, of a tragic event. I doubt she has ever mentioned it to her mother and father. Observe this speeding ticket I am holding up now. I will take the liberty of reading it: "State of New York, County of Onondaga. Name: Virginia

Wood. Kansas address. And a fine of $150 for driving ninety miles an hour in a sixty-five-miles-an-hour zone on the New York State Thruway.

"I must apologize to Virginia and her family because I had a good deal to do with the incident. I am a major dealer of Chevrolets and am ranked in the public's eye at the lowest possible level—below lawyers, doctors, funeral directors, and garbage collectors. I have three franchises in Western New York.

"The day I met Virginia, I happened to be driving one of my Corvettes, a demo, but a real beauty with five forward gears. Virginia took a look at it and asked if she could give it a try. I taught her how to drive the car: how to double clutch, how to down shift, and most of all, how to take a sharp corner as fast as she could.

"She had a great time learning, and I was so impressed that I loaned another car to her and her Larry for the drive he took her on, all around beautiful Western New York—down Lake Erie, to Chautauqua, over to Cornell Law School in Ithaca, and then due north on the New York State Thruway for the trip back to Rochester. Dear Virginia blasted through a state police radar trap at one hundred miles per hour, as evidenced by this speeding ticket."

As he spoke, Ginny buried her face in her hands, but Rufus continued.

"The fact is, Mrs. Larry Pace loves fast cars."

And with that, Rufus turned, and walked to the far corner of the tent, where he briefly disappeared. Suddenly we heard a thunderous roar as he slowly drove into the tent a brand new Chevrolet Corvette, midnight blue with red leather interior. He stopped it right in front of Ginny and me, got out of the car, and said, "Virginia, here is the title to this gorgeous car and two sets of keys."

He handed the keys to Ginny.

I had never before seen her gob smacked. She stood up and exclaimed "Uncle Rufus! I wish I could say 'You shouldn't have,' but I'm not giving these back"—and she snatched the keys from him.

Rufus replied, "There are two sets of keys. Are you going to give one to Larry?"

"I'll have to think that over," she said, into the microphone, "but Larry dear, I wouldn't count on it."

The crowd jumped up laughing and cheering.

Rufus's magnificent gift was one of many we received during the reception. After he sat down, my father and mother stood up to take the microphone. My father introduced himself. "I am Larry's father. Like all of the other members of our family, I was so happy to meet Virginia and experience her warmth and kind heart." He handed the microphone to my mother, who continued, "Let me begin with a story of Larry's great grandfather. He mined gold in Alaska during the great gold rush in 1898. When he came home, he had some of the gold made into an engagement ring, which he gave to Larry's great grandmother when he bent on one knee and asked her to marry him. He went on to build the jewelry businesses that Jason and I have run for years, but when our darling daughter-in-law-to-be visited us in Rochester, I gave that ring to Larry and said, 'I get the feeling this may come in handy soon.'"

The crowd began to clap. My mother passed the microphone back to my father, who then said cheerily, in a tone I have always enjoyed, "We also have several travel agencies located in the greater Rochester area." He held up a large white envelope tied with a gold ribbon and bow. My mother took the envelope and walked to the dais where, standing on tip toe, she handed the envelope up to Ginny.

Ginny looked at it for a few seconds, untied the ribbon, and took out a large letter, which she unfolded. After a pause, she looked up at the crowd and said, "Please let me read you this letter: 'Dearest Mr. and Mrs. Pace—Our wedding presents to you are the attached two credit cards, creating separate accounts for each of you. The cards are open ended and may be used by you to pay for whatever you want to do on your honeymoon. We mean *everything*—meals, first-class travel, five-star hotels, and absolutely anything else you can imagine wanting or needing. *Do not stint yourselves!* Love and safe journey, Mom and Dad.'"

I saw small tears in Ginny's eyes. She took a deep breath, and looking straight at my parents, she said with great force, "Jason and Mildred, I have never felt more welcomed and wanted. You will be my other mom and my dad, just as I know my parents will be the same for Larry. Thank you both. I am deeply indebted to you and will remain so to the end of my life."

It was a fantastic reception. Ginny and I didn't get to bed until about 1:30 in the morning, when we made love for the first time. I looked down at her, kissed her again and again, then said, "I'm amazed, sweetheart. For a lady who has never done this before, you did pretty damn well!"

"Sweetheart," she said, "my desire for you has always been a ticking time bomb, and finally I could explode. Just because

I saved myself for you doesn't mean I have not wanted to go the distance before. Some of my girlfriends who were saving themselves didn't have to wait very long. Some married at twenty or twenty-one, but I turned down several good men whom I did not love, so, my time bomb has been ticking for about seven years!"

We had another round and then another, and then we woke up bleary eyed from lack of sleep at 7:00 in the morning because we had to pack for our honeymoon, have breakfast downstairs with our few remaining guests, and catch the hotel shuttle to the airport.

We made it to the airport in plenty of time and boarded our flight to New York, using first-class reservations for that flight and our anticipated non-stop flight to Madrid.

CHAPTER
34

Ginny and I had often talked about the honeymoon we wanted. We both wished to go to several great museums—the Met in New York, the Prado in Madrid, the Louvre in Paris, and the cluster of museums in the Netherlands where we could see the Vermeers, Rembrandts, and Van Goghs. Ginny also wanted to meet significant librarians in each city.

Since neither of us could get away from work for more than three weeks, not nearly enough for deep visits to these museums as well as Ginny's appointments with librarians, we agreed to spend just a few days in each city. This would give us a chance to learn which we'd like to return to in later years.

In New York, thanks to my parents, we stayed in the exclusive Ritz-Carlton Hotel, only two blocks away from the Metropolitan Museum 'and Central Park, where we could easily jog. We arrived at the hotel late in the afternoon and were promptly shown to our huge bedroom on the eighth floor. We had a beautiful view of Central Park, east to west and north to south. We settled in with a bath for Ginny and a shower for me, after which we were too tired to find a nearby restaurant. We called in reservations at the hotel's five-star dining room, where we were met by a maître d', who identified himself as Claude. He greeted us warmly and led us to a small table in the far corner, a kind of private nook.

I have always loved eating out and paying attention to how restaurants are managed. As I watched the waitstaff and sommeliers serve their customers, I knew at first glance that it was a well-run restaurant. There were no dining tables anywhere near the door to the kitchen, so all the diners could eat without the intrusive noise of the kitchen door opening and slamming shut, the sounds of the chefs shouting, the clank of dinner plates, and the splashing sounds of the dishwashing.

Back in our room, we were too exhausted to do anything more than wash up, brush and floss our teeth, gargle, strip off our clothes, and slide between the cool, satin sheets of our king-size bed. We lay our heads on the goose down pillows and spooned together peacefully as we drifted softly into a deep sleep.

The next day, we headed to the Met. We paid our entry fees, got our visitors' stickers, and made reservations for lunch in the trustee's dining room, which my cousin Pamela, a long-time New Yorker, had recommended as one of the lesser known culinary gems of the city.

After spending the first day enjoying some of the staggering collections of the Met, we went the next morning to the executive office of the New York City Public Library, where we met Seymour Kaufman, the director of the city's library system. He and Ginny had met before. He gave us extraordinary attention as he showed Ginny how the huge library system was actually run. We saw the work rooms where books were repaired, the offices where important acquisition decisions were made, the library's computing system, and last, but certainly not least, the temperature-controlled vault in the basement where priceless books and manuscripts were made available only to accredited scholars.

As we moved through the huge facility, I walked behind Mr. Kaufman and Ginny, reveling in the immense pleasure Ginny was experiencing as she talked shop with the director. Her system was small compared to his, but she was, after all, the chief librarian of the Kansas City Public Library system. In no way was he condescending. They both loved books and cared very much how library books are chosen and how they are treated. Theirs was a conversation between professionals.

Ginny and I spent the next day walking through Central Park, an extraordinary haven in the middle of the huge metropolis. At six o'clock, a car service the concierge had kindly arranged for us took us to Kennedy International Airport for our flight to Spain.

As we got out of the car at the airport, an attractive older woman in an Iberia Airlines uniform approached us. She introduced herself as Aviva.

"Good evening, Mr. and Mrs. Pace," she said. "It is a pleasure to have you join us for Flight 1005, leaving at 10:00 and arriving in Madrid tomorrow morning. We will try to make your trip as comfortable as possible, so please follow me." She started to lead us into the terminal, at which point another Iberian employee scooped up our luggage and loaded it onto a cart.

Aviva led us through the crowds to two thick glass doors

set in gleaming stainless steel, each with a mahogany handle. She punched an entry code into a square lock, and with a sharp click, the doors opened as gracefully and smoothly as the doors of a bank vault. As they closed behind us, we saw stretching before us a vast space: a lounge luxuriously appointed with seats upholstered in Spanish leather, dining tables, two bars, and a fireplace. At this point, I suddenly fully understood the magnitude of my parents' gift. For the first time in our lives, we had entered an airport without having to lug our own suitcases or stand in long check-in lines. It was mind boggling.

Aviva described the facilities, saying, "We also have a few single and double bedrooms where passengers can sleep whenever they feel the need." I glanced at Ginny, and she at me, and then we stepped into the promised land of air travel.

After leisurely enjoying a five-course meal, we boarded the plane with six other first-class passengers. Aviva warmly greeted us again, smiling, and directed us to our seats, which were nearly as wide as twin beds. She made sure we had correctly fastened our seatbelts, then, while we waited for the "lesser" passengers to board, she served us glasses of wine and light hors d'oeuvres of warm buns spread with cream cheese and covered with caviar.

There followed a gourmet dinner of three courses with fine wines. Unfortunately, because we'd had an even better dinner in the lounge, we could manage just two courses of this new meal. Once the dinner was complete and we'd had our cognac, Aviva came with another cabin attendant. Asking us politely to stand up, they quickly converted the seats into a spacious, nearly queen-size bed.

Ginny and I looked at each other. Neither of us could believe our eyes. Our two hearts pumped out thank you messages to my parents. But as if that was not enough, the other flight attendant, Dorthea, informed us that we were welcome to use the shower room at the head of first-class seating.

"How did you fit a shower room in here?!" Ginny exclaimed.

"Well, it is not a room, but there is space for one person to stand and wash yourself, towel off, and get dressed. It is a bit cramped."

"Is there room for two?" I asked, smiling widely.

Dorthea looked me right in the eyes and said, "No sir, there is only room for one person." And then, with an appropriate twinkle in her eyes, she said, "I'm not even sure there is room for you alone!"

We each opted out of the shower, climbed into bed, kissed and hugged, and settled into our usual spooning. For the first time in our lives, we actually slept on a plane.

CHAPTER
35

n Madrid, at the Prado, Ginny and I were both bowled over by the variety of paintings, sculptures, and Islamic tiles. We appreciated the warmth and kindness with which our requests for suggestions of good places to eat were received, and we enjoyed the Paseo, the stroll that the Spanish take every evening. We also enjoyed lots of *tapas* earlier in the day.

The next morning, we were off to Paris. As the plane descended at Charles DeGaulle, we could see stretched before us the vast city—the avenues, boulevards, and bridges. It had been Ginny's turn for the window seat, so she got the better view of the stunning City of Lights.

Sophisticated travelers to France know that one does best if one can speak French, even if haltingly, because the French, perhaps more than any of the other Europeans, experience their language as a culture. In our case, we knew enough of the basics to get around, and we enjoyed the flashes of pleasure we occasionally saw in their faces as we did our best to speak.

Almost as important as speaking French, is ensuring that a French taxi driver does not rip you off. When we got into a cab, I took the lead because I could speak a little better than Ginny. I went back and forth with the driver regarding the fees, which were governed by municipal law and set forth clearly on the car's meter. However, as I expected, when I handed our payment to the cabbie in francs, having included a reasonable tip, he feigned deep disappointment and said, in French, "How can one even run a cab on such a small tip?!" But I had no intention of handing him more.

Experienced visitors to the Louvre describe it as overwhelming. Some say that it is not possible, even in one's lifetime, to see all of the masterpieces in that hallowed place, so Ginny and I decided to spend our two days looking at just a few of the galleries that held some of our favorite paintings.

On the third day, we met Sylvie de Range, the chief librarian of the city. The library tour she gave us was, for Ginny, as exciting and engaging as the others had been. As had happened with the library director in Madrid, the conversation consisted of intense shop talk focused on the complexities of various issues—how to set and collect library fines, as well as the criteria for selecting new purchases on a limited budget. At the end of the tour, Sylvie invited us to join her and her husband at what she said was one of Paris' finest restaurants, all at the library's expense.

At eight o'clock that evening, we stepped out of our taxi in front of Montard's, where we met Sylvie and her husband George. He was a restaurant critic for *Paris Match* and was wearing a deep blue, obviously made-to-measure suit, probably from Savile Row, and a shiny, gold wrist watch. He was a true, Parisian boulevardier, but as he extended his hand, his smile was genuine.

George looked me in the eye and said, "It is with great pleasure that I meet you, Larry, and your lovely bride Ginny. Sylvie told me you and she had a marvelous time together running about in the hidden nooks and crannies of the Paris library offices. She also told me of your interest in art and that you, Larry, are an *avocat.* In English, I think that is a 'lawyer'? So I look forward to hearing about your exciting cases of murder and mayhem."

The restaurant was casually chic, with a dozen dark leather booths, each seating four, and the same number of tables. With an elegant extension of his arm, the waiter directed us to our table, which was beautifully set, with a bottle of Perrier at each place. Sylvie explained that there was only a prix-fixe menu of five courses. "Each course is small," she said, "compared to the huge plates of food I was given in your restaurants in America, but the key point here is to taste. And may I respectfully suggest that the best way to taste is to take small bites, chew completely, and listen to your tongue?"

When all was said and done, and Ginny and I were in the taxi heading back to our hotel, we talked about how we'd never before had the kinds of elegant foods that were served in the restaurant, and how there were no diversions from the tastes, as there were in American restaurants. The experience changed how we thought about food and how we ate, and it has influenced us to this day.

We left for the Netherlands the next day, and our visit there proved to be the most rewarding of our honeymoon. The Dutch were cordial and most of them spoke perfect English. They enjoyed the beauty around them—the acres of multi-colored tulips, the elegant facades of the buildings lining their streets (many of which dated back to the seventeenth century and William of Orange), their canals—all arranged in an orderly, yet charming way.

Most important, once Ginny and I got to the museums, we found huge collections of Vermeers, Van Goghs, and lesser Dutch masters. The paintings took my breath away.

One of the guides at the museum where we saw the most Vermeers told us a story of the criminal trials held at the International Criminal Court after the Balkan Wars. For months, day in and day out, the judges were presented with photographs, movies, and testimony regarding the appalling slaughter that the Serbian soldiers had committed against their Balkan neighbors. At the end of a long day, the judges often came to the museum to sit quietly and enjoy the gorgeous humanity of Vermeer's paintings. They used this as a means to calm themselves after all they had heard during the day.

Changing planes at Kennedy as we headed for Kansas City on our return home, , I knew that our honeymoon, built around beauty and our respect for books and learning, had been the best we ever could have had. This made our re-entry even more traumatic. We settled into our home—my modest house—but went straight back to work. Ginny had catching up to do at the library and I returned to my desk at the office, which was covered with papers.

Before I could begin, Arleen waylaid me, put a soft hand on my cheek and asked, "How was the honeymoon?" I looked straight in her eyes, my own eyes moistening slightly, and said, "Beyond my wildest dreams!"

She turned to her desk and handed me another stack of

files. "Welcome back to the real world," she said. It was a huge pile of papers, but, as she always had, Arleen had arranged the documents efficiently, clipping to each a brief explanation of the most urgent issues.

Ginny and I had recognized that I would need to stay late each night during the first week or so of our return in order for me to grind through the files awaiting my attention. The quid pro quo was that Ginny had free reign to arrange and decorate our house.

A couple of months later, when I slid into bed next to her at midnight, Ginny rolled over, kissed me, and said, "Sweetheart, I missed my period."

After this sank in, I asked, "Are you pregnant?"

"I'm not sure," she said. "I have an appointment with my gynecologist on Tuesday, and we'll find out then."

CHAPTER
36

Ginny was pregnant—with twins, no less! After she told me, we sat together on the sofa holding hands, speechless.

"Well," I said. "This changes things!"

"You think?!" she replied.

After a long pause, she squeezed my hand more tightly.

"Darling," I said, "I'm so happy that now is the time we're starting our family. Otherwise, when we finally finished producing five, we'd look like their grandparents—not their mom and dad."

I kissed her. We both stood up and hugged each other firmly. With tears beginning to roll down her cheeks, she put her hands around my neck, looked into my eyes, and said, "Dearest, thank you, thank you, thank you. This is the family I have dreamed of since I was a little girl, and God willing there will be at least three more after these two!"

Then, with a teasing twinkle in her brown eyes, she added, "Or perhaps more?"

"I would not be included in any such effort!" I said. "But let's talk about names now—boys names and girls names."

We decided on "Sarah," a name Ginny had always loved, and "James," after my great grandfather, James Kelley, who had mined the gold for the engagement ring I'd given to Ginny.

It must have been God's loving grace that Ginny's pregnancy went off without a hitch. She was rarely severely uncomfortable and hardly experienced any morning sickness. The twins put in their appearance right on schedule in the middle of the ninth month, almost bursting out—first one, followed immediately by the other. The photo I took of her holding them both was perfect. She was exhausted but managed a slight smile.

Because this was her first pregnancy and she'd had twins, the doctors decided to keep Ginny under observation in the hospital for a week or so. When we finally got home with our babies, their room was ready for them. We decided to put them in the same crib initially, to see how that would work.

There followed weeks of babies crying endlessly and ear piercingly, sometimes minutes, sometimes longer. I was struck by how the babies did not seem to mind us lifting up their feet and butts, removing their soiled diapers, cleaning them, and re-diapering them—and they began to look straight at us as we changed them, over and over. They were perhaps beginning to recognize us, I thought.

Ginny nursed the babies whenever they cried, and we eventually settled into a routine, deciding who would get up in the middle of the night to change them, who would bottle feed them (once Ginny stopped nursing), and who would wash and boil their diapers.

Chapter 36

We were both exhausted. I'd had to go back to work right after Ginny had come home from the hospital. Ginny could sleep while the babies were napping, but I was back at my desk without having ever had a full night of sleep. I managed each day with Arleen's help.

Ginny enjoyed Sarah and Jimmy and was healthy and happy. When I saw how absorbed she was in rearing our kids, I asked, "How about if you don't go back to work? We don't really need the money. I can always put in a few more hours at the firm. And you'll get to do what you always dreamed of—raise a family." It took Ginny less than a nano-second for her to reply, "You're right, dear. Thank you. That's exactly what I'm going to do."

CHAPTER
37

And so, we grew our family. The second set of twins, Jackson and Grace, made their appearance three years later. Several months after that, Marty Logue came into my office and settled into my beautiful, overstuffed, deep green leather sofa. It was made nearly forty years before by the Gunlocke Furniture Company and was slightly cracked in places with age. My grandfather had given it to me when I passed the bar in Missouri.

Settling into the end furthest from my desk, Marty, as usual, opened the conversation with his favorite platitudes. "How are you? How's Ginny doing? Boy, the four kids must be running you ragged."

Finally, he cut to the chase. "Larry, you may have heard rumors, but a couple of nights ago, the senior partners voted unanimously to open an office in D.C. and to make you a senior partner, as of now—whether you like it or not! We want to make you head of that office because you are now a senior partner and you are the only person in the firm who has regularly handled our business in Washington. You've appeared before the U.S. Circuit Court of Appeals for D.C., stood before regulatory agencies, and filed a petition for a writ of certiorari to the Supreme Court. You got three votes out of nine—not enough to get you the writ, but still something all of us in the firm admired. Of course, this is in addition to your appearances before the Second Circuit in Manhattan, the Eighth Circuit in St. Louis, and the Supreme Courts of Missouri and Kansas! We want you in D.C. in seven days or so, and . . ."

"What the hell are you talking about, Marty?! I can't possibly move my family halfway across the country in a week or ten days! I'll have to convince Ginny and I don't think she'll stand for it."

"Jesus Christ, Larry, we're not stupid! Of course we've already talked with Ginny. Grace Borman and I spoke with her yesterday afternoon. She had some questions, but she said she'd have no problem getting the kids and *you* onto the Gulf Stream this coming Friday for a non-stop flight to Washington."

All I could do was sit there aghast.

"What the hell did you offer her?" I asked.

"Well, Larry, my dear friend and colleague, I have even greater respect for you—or perhaps concern—after talking with Ginny. I don't think I've ever met a more powerful, bare knuckles negotiator. Where did she ever learn how to do it?"

"Mainly by mercilessly enforcing library fines and canceling the library cards of people who were delinquent," I explained.

"Anyway," Marty continued, "there will be a car at your house at 9:00 am on Saturday to take you to the airport.

Chapter 37

Ginny was particularly tough on that point. I wanted to get you on the plane no later than 7:30 so you'd reach D.C. by noon, but she said no because of the need to get the kids up and dressed.

"She was toughest on how you'd live in D.C. We proposed a short-term lease of a small bungalow in Arlington. She countered with a demand for a two-week stay in the penthouse of the Four Seasons Hotel so your family would be comfortable while you and she looked for housing. She particularly emphasized the hotel's Olympic-sized swimming pool for your kids. Although Ginny and I were talking on the phone, I kept having a vision of her leaning across a negotiating table, eyes wide and focused, her tone stern, while she jabbed her finger in the air at me. Bottom line, she got everything she wanted and a little more—the penthouse, fully paid tuition for private schools, and a designated realtor—John Callandar—to help you find a suitable house."

"My God, how would she get the name of a realtor?" I asked.

After a deep sigh, Marty said, "Arleen, of course."

Then he added, "Speaking of that human whirlwind, one of Ginny's implacable negotiating points was that if Arleen and Oscar were amenable, they would go with you to D.C. I wish I could tell you that the firm was already thinking of asking them to move with you, but truth be told, it was Ginny's idea, the *only* thing that we didn't have to negotiate. It made beautiful sense all round. I'd completely forgotten that Oscar was born and grew up in D.C. He has numerous contacts and family there who may be able to funnel clients to our new office, and he and Arleen are happy to move."

Marty stood up and walked across the huge expanse of my office. He sat in one of the chairs directly in front of my enormous desk. Leaning forward and fixing me with kind eyes, he said, "My close negotiations with your wife sealed in my own mind the conviction that you would be the best member of the firm to run our new office. This wasn't because of Ginny's take-no-prisoners negotiating tactics but because it was very clear to me that everything she was demanding grew from the deep and enduring love in her heart for you. So I want to be clear, speaking for the senior partners and myself, we have deep affection for you. You are a good person, which, at the end of the day, is what we want every person in this firm to be."

We stood up and shook hands, firmly and warmly.

Then, as he left, Marty turned and said, "So, your working career at this particular office is over as of now. Go home and get your family ready for the big trip. *Anything* you and your family need during this transition, you come first to me!"

CHAPTER
38

O
n Friday morning, Ginny tried hurriedly to finish getting the kids packed. This involved significant negotiations with each concerning which stuffed animals they could take on the plane. The suitcases were on the floor.

"I want my doll," Sarah said.

"My frog!" Jimmy added.

The kids directed the packing of the remainder of their animals and dolls into the suitcases.

Jimmy was an aviation enthusiast, and he exploded in excitement when he heard me say that we would be flying in a Gulfstream. "Dad, is this a Gulfstream G600 or a Gulfstream G700? If it's a G700, it can cruise at 40,000 feet." He whipped out a pocket calculator. "That would mean it would take exactly four hours and fifty-eight minutes to get to Washington!"

Jimmy knew that the firm would have had to choose a particular interior after it had bought the Gulfstream—seats and an aisle, or a galley, a couch? What would the firm have chosen? Fortunately, his ruminations on these points did not impede the packing, and we were ready, with a steamer trunk, two large suitcases, and a small suitcase each for Jimmy and Sarah.

"What about the furniture?" I asked.

"Nothing to fear, my darling, handsome, senior partner."

And at that, there was a loud honk. We began lugging the baggage out of the house and into the van for our ride to the airport.

When we approached Kansas City International Airport, Jimmy got very upset, thinking we had missed our exit. He was ecstatic, somehow bouncing up and down on his seat, despite his tight-fitting seatbelt, when the driver took the next exit and stopped at the curb by All American Private Flying Services. The driver held open the doors and the baggage handlers from All American took charge. We were welcomed into the building by an elegant concierge who invited us to have breakfast in the lounge, saying, "Please take your time. We fly only when *you* are ready to fly!"

Jimmy was ready to fly right then and there, but he did a one-hundred-eighty degree turn when he saw the vast buffet before us: eggs made to order, salads and meats, and at the very end of the line, pancakes. Jimmy and Sarah made a beeline for the pancakes. Jimmy looked up at the chef and asked, "How many pancakes do you cook for each person?"

"See these four griddles?" the cook answered. "The pancake batter is in this little bag, just like frosting for a cake, and I can cook you any number, any size."

Jimmy gave his order: "Sixteen, please, with butter and maple syrup in between each one."

I made it to the chef before he could start and said, "Just four, medium large, please."

Chapter 38

"Golly, that's too bad! I really wanted to see if I could cook sixteen pancakes at a time," the chef teased.

Somehow, we got all the food that everyone wanted. As we headed to the beautifully appointed, dark, hardwood tables, waiters quickly brought two high chairs for the youngest twins and two kids' chairs for the older ones, leaving two grown up chairs for Ginny and me.

The kids ate their food as kids do. Ginny and I had to feed Jackson and Grace while eating our own breakfasts. Jimmy took one look at the Vermont Maple syrup and asked, "Do you have any Log Cabin syrup?"

"Jimmy!" Ginny was embarrassed by our son's pickiness.

The waiter did not bat an eyelash. "We certainly do, young man," he said, then turned to Ginny. "It's no problem at all, madam. We get requests like this all the time and we're ready for anything."

"Thank you very much," Ginny said. "We greatly appreciate your patience."

In what seemed like a split second, a bottle of Log Cabin was on the table. We all finished our breakfasts, which for Ginny and me had included toasted muffins topped with cream cheese and caviar (Ginny had grown to like it), cereal, juice, and coffee. At the end of the meal, Ginny took Grace, Sarah, and Jackson to the women's room for diapers and a bathroom break. I took Jimmy to the men's room.

Finally, we were ready. The concierge led us out the door to where the Gulfstream was waiting, its steps down. Jimmy leapt up the stairs. Sarah was more cautious. Ginny and I followed, holding Jackson and Grace.

As the pilot turned the luxurious private jet onto the takeoff runway, he locked the brakes, and slowly increased thrust for takeoff. As the plane started to shudder, he unlocked the brakes and we shot down the runway like an arrow from a bow. After what seemed to me to be no takeoff run at all, the pilot rotated sharply and quickly got us to our cruising altitude at forty thousand feet. We were on our way to D.C. at an airspeed of 650 miles per hour and a ground speed of just over five hundred miles an hour.

We landed at Washington National and pulled to a full stop at the All American terminal in less than two hours. A car service met us and within forty-five minutes, we were walking into the door of our penthouse.

CHAPTER

39

Our temporary penthouse home was almost completely glass-walled, with spectacular views of the city, particularly to the west, where we saw flat land all the way to the horizon. Each set of twins had their own bedrooms, and we had a master bedroom with a large dressing room and two bathrooms.

My first thought was, *I'm not moving out of here no matter how many houses the realtor shows us!*

The phone next to the bed rang and I picked it up. It was the concierge telling us that the hotel could provide us with baby sitters for the kids if we wanted them. Ginny thought that would be fine for the older twins, but she wanted to look out for the younger ones herself. The kids took their naps and Ginny and I had a brief lie-down until two o'clock, when the realtor arrived.

He turned out to be an older African American man. The three of us sat down at the dining table, where he showed us a large map of the metropolitan area, with the boundary lines of cities and towns clearly marked.

"Thank you so much, Mr. Callander, for coming to us, rather than asking us to come to you," Ginny said. "We're interested in the neighborhoods around Georgetown Day School and Sidwell Friends, since we're thinking of either of those schools for the kids. We'd like to see homes near those schools."

"I certainly can certainly show you some, ma'am," Mr. Callander replied. "Those neighborhoods are very attractive. There's also the National Cathedral School, but that takes only girls, and I suspect you want the young ones to be together."

"Yes, yes," Ginny replied quickly. "We have two sets of twins—a boy and a girl in both cases. The oldest two are six and the younger are only two. We prefer co-ed schools that start at kindergarten and continue through twelfth grade. I'm wondering what you think of the two schools I've mentioned."

"Well, ma'am, I went to Georgetown Day School from ninth grade. I liked it a lot but I don't know if you're aware that Sidwell is run by Quakers. In my opinion, it is the very best school in this area of the type you're looking for—with one drawback. At Sidwell there are a lot kids of VIPs, so there are security needs sometimes. You might see Secret Service agents (Sidwell is very good at providing a safe environment), but there are kids with no need for security, as well."

I spotted a twinkle in Mr. Callander's eyes—the beginning of a smile. "I should tell you that Georgetown beat the heck out of Sidwell in sports, which is what I spent a lot of time doing there." He briefly chuckled.

"Well," I said, glancing at Ginny. "We'd like it if you would show us homes in each area."

Chapter 39

"I'd be very happy to do that right now if it's convenient for you."

We spent the rest of the afternoon and a good part of the next day with Realtor Callander, and by 6:30 on the second day, we had a signed contract for a beautiful, six-bedroom home within walking distance of Sidwell Friends. It was pricey, but I knew that it was precisely what the firm wanted for us. It gave Ginny and me access to the families of Sidwell students, many of whom were businesspeople, lawyers, and politicos. Sidwell was a client-rich environment.

We stayed in the hotel until we closed on the house. As we turned the key to the door of our new home, the moving van pulled up with our furniture. Within a couple of hours, we were enjoying a beautifully furnished and appointed home.

The following week, I called Mr. Callander for help looking into office spaces. It took three weeks to find the right place. I sent the lease to Marty for review before I signed it. As it turned out, Mr. Callander had one last feather in his cap. "Attorney Pace," he said as he handed me a business card, "I also have a large furniture rental company here in D.C. I offer a range of the finest furniture for professional offices. I can lease you all the furniture you need—it's the highest quality and of the sort your clients would expect. You get new furniture every three years, billed at the going rate."

Mr. Callander had been right about the neighborhoods and the schools, so he was surely right about the furniture. "Can you show me a catalogue of what you offer?" I asked.

"That I can do," he said. "How about if we meet tomorrow morning to take a look?"

"That's good. Bring a copy of your lease agreement, too, ok?"

"You bet," he said. "Say we meet here at 9:30 or 10:00 tomorrow?"

I agreed, and we talked the next day, but it took about a month to get everything set up—the desks, the library, the reception area. Once we were done, we welcomed our first clients. Within the next few months, the place was humming with new business and lots of money—just as Marty had hoped—and it was no longer necessary for me to work the brutal, long hours of the past. I left that kind of work to my five, long-suffering associates.

One evening, I got home exhausted about eleven. I joined Ginny in bed, where she had been waiting for me. We cuddled close, and she whispered, "Our fifth child is on the way, sweetheart!"

"*And* our last!" I said, as I kissed her on the nose.

Eight months later, Beverly was born.

CHAPTER
40

About six months later, on a gorgeous spring day, Ginny and I were walking with our brood along Tyson Road in Alexandria. Ginny was walking in front with Beverly strapped to her chest. She was holding Sarah with her right hand and Jimmy with her left. I pushed the younger twins, Grace and Jackson, in a double stroller.

As we crossed the street, we came upon a large construction site stretching a full block. It was guarded by a ten-foot chain link fence and tall boards that surrounded the pit dug for the base of the skyscraper. There was a narrow driveway between the construction site and a trailer used as an on-site office.

As we approached the trailer, the door opened and Dell Bondi stepped out and down the steps to the sidewalk. She turned toward us, stopped, stunned, and called out, "Larry!"

"Dell! After all these years!" I exclaimed.

That instant, Ginny assumed her rampart position, stood ram rod straight and snarled, "What are *you* doing here?"

To the average bystander, it was obvious: a citizen was

about to walk lawfully down the street, minding her own business, but of course that is not what Ginny thought. If I knew Ginny, and I did, she was afraid of Dell being a home-wrecker—the old flame with her sexy charms might lure me away from my family.

There was just a moment's time before Dell spoke. She said exactly what she needed to say. She told her story.

"*Mrs.* Pace," she said. Many years ago, in Kansas City, Larry and I spent a long weekend together at my house, and we fell in love. A very deep love. A love I had never, ever before felt from a man.

"I grew up in an orphanage. I was never told who my parents were. I was just found in a little basket, wrapped in a blanket, on the doorstep.

"The nuns made us feel bad, telling us how sinful we were and how no one would ever love us. When I got older, I ended up with two foster parents, then a second couple, then a third. None of them really cared about me. They just wanted the money they got from the state for their being foster parents. Two of the men mistreated me badly."

I thought it clear what she meant, but she wasn't going to speak explicitly in the presence of the children.

"So, going to bed at night was pretty scary," she continued.

"Then, when I was eighteen and aged out of foster care, I met my parents. Not my biological parents, because I never knew who they were, but the people who took me in and later adopted me—John and Milly Bondi. They let me live in their house. I had my own room. I had never had space of my own before.

"When I started barricading my room so no one could

get in at night, my mom asked why. It took months of their good food and warmth, of being loved by them, going to church with them, and evenings of being helped with my homework for the GED program before I could trust them. Even after several years with my wonderful mom and dad, I still had flashbacks, and I'd wake up screaming in the middle of the night. My parents would come in and hold me in their arms until I could fall asleep.

"My dad was a soldier in the war and told me about what they called 'battle fatigue.' Today, it's 'PTSD.' He said that's what I had. Living with various foster parents, I had been in a war zone—men abusing me, the wives not stopping it—but at church I was taught about God's love. The priest gave me a little prayer book called *Jesus Calling,* which I still have today, all dog eared."

I glanced at Ginny. She had resumed her normal posture, bending slightly toward Dell and completely focused on her.

"Mom and Dad had lots of books in their house," Dell continued. "Once, I found a big one, with pictures of buildings. I'll bet you've seen them—full of photos of skyscrapers. I couldn't believe how the workers were able to build those skyscrapers with I-beams and rivets, from the first floor to the top. I marveled at the pictures of them throwing hot rivets from one to another and sitting casually on the I-beams eating their lunches, high above the city.

"I became obsessed. I talked about those photos all the time until Mom and Dad got a little concerned and took me to a therapist. I learned from him what everything meant. The hidden meaning was that as the buildings got taller and taller, they took me out of the world of my fears to a world where the fears did not exist, where I could do anything I wanted to do.

"Eventually, Mom and Dad sent me to Rensselaer Polytechnic Institute in New York, where I spent four years learning construction engineering. I loved every minute at RPI. I couldn't stay out of the library. The school even took us to the city to see complex construction underway. Six years later, I graduated with a master's degree.

"When I got back to Kansas City, back home, my parents gave me my graduation present. They took me to the bank and showed me the safe deposit box where they had kept $250,000, mainly in bonds, though there was some cash."

"'This money is for you,' they said. 'We have loved you so much, and you have returned that love. We've talked to our lawyers. They can set up a construction engineering company for you. All this will cost a lot of money. We want you to have everything in this box so you can get started on the great life ahead of you, doing what you love.'"

"I couldn't help myself," Dell said. "I sat at the little table where we'd put the deposit box and sobbed and sobbed. I had a vision that Jesus was with me. But now," she added, with a little twinkle in her eye, "I'm also thinking that not even Jesus could have gotten into that vault."

"The next day, my parents took me to see Martin Logue at Clauson, Schwarz, and Logue. He set everything up—all the papers that I needed for my corporation—and I rented a little bungalow where I had my first office and where I slept. Marty gave my name to various potential clients and before I knew it, I was going great guns. I had a good reputation for getting jobs done on budget and on time, but that's all I did.

"I was just getting really started when I met you, Larry. I fell in love with you. I had never known the kind of love I experienced with you. And you know what? No PTSD."

She took a deep breath and looked me right in the eye. "Larry, I should never have left you the way I did. I should have explained. I knew that if I stayed with you, if we married, if we had children, I could not also build my buildings, so I just left. Larry, I am so, so sorry for leaving you without a word. You loved me so deeply and so well, and I pushed you away."

Her voice trembled. "Please forgive me. I know I can never make it up to you, but please forgive me."

"Of course, Dell," I said. "That was a long time ago. I'm so happy for you—for what you've done with your life."

"Yes," she said. "If you look through that little opening in the fence, you'll see what I do."

Jimmy and I looked through the fence. We were amazed. There was a deep, deep pit. We could see some concrete and the first bit of scaffolding. Clearly, Dell was the owner of a major corporation.

Dell went on. "The only problem is that I have left no room for a family. But look at you, Larry! Look at your beautiful family! You have a lovely wife and five children who have everything they need."

Ginny said softly, "Well, that's not exactly right. See this little one?" She slowly took Beverly from the front carrier. "See this little bundle of joy? Her name is Beverly." The baby, on cue, started to gurgle. "Dell," Ginny continued, "Beverly says she wants you to be her godmother. She does not have one."

Dell was speechless. Ginny took Beverly, wrapped in a little blanket, and handed her to Dell, who gingerly held out her arms.

"It's easy," Ginny said. "Just put your hands under her bottom and her head. Keep her head supported."

Dell held Beverly in her arms. The baby reached up and grabbed a handful of Dell's hair, which was now lightly streaked with gray.

"You see, Dell," Ginny said, "she's asking if you will be her godmother," and right on time, Beverly looked in her eyes and gurgled again.

Dell looked up, eyes, moistening. "I would just love it. What do I do?"

"You show up at her christening, birthday parties, Christmas, Thanksgiving and other holidays if you can. If, God forbid, something happened to Larry and me, you would be responsible for seeing that she would be taken care of. Believe me when I say I have absolutely no doubt that this little baby will always be safe in your arms."

Dell held the baby a little longer, and we talked. As she passed Beverly back to us, I glanced down the alley, past the construction trailer, and thought I saw the nose of Dell's MG.

"Dell! Do you still have your old MG?"

"A sportscar?" Jimmy yelled, and started down the alley at top speed. We followed him, and there it was—the green MG, with yellow, leather upholstery. For just a flash, I saw Dell as I had seen her long ago, turning the car and waving her hand.

Uninvited, Jimmy vaulted over the door and into the passenger seat. "Dell! Can you give me a ride? Please? Please."

"Only if your mom says, ok, Jimmy."

Ginny smiled and nodded, and they were off.

About half an hour later, I heard in the distance the throaty roar of the MG. The sound got louder and louder as Dell downshifted, then she rounded the corner and brought the vintage car to a soft stop.

Jimmy jumped over the side of the car, and started talking at an excited, machine-gun-like pace. "Mom! Guess what? Guess what we did?!"

He described the streets and curves, the upshifting and downshifting. As he yelled in joy, Ginny and I looked at each other, both thinking, *What a marvelous, joyful, free-spirited little boy.*

Dell apologized. "I'm sorry. I really have to get back to work. But I am so glad we bumped into each other. We need to keep in close touch!"

We exchanged business cards and phone numbers, and she got into her car and pulled into her parking space, then she got out and disappeared into the trailer.

CHAPTER
41

Over the next few years, our family settled into D.C. The firm's D.C. office was extremely profitable, and our kids grew and thrived. They had occasional meltdowns, and Ginny and I had our moments of tension. Our firm gained many clients and sometimes lost a few, and we had to have a few conferences with teachers—particularly regarding Jackson—but all in all, life was very good.

True to her promise, Dell made sure to come to Beverly's christening, where she was made the baby's godmother. She regularly sent birthday presents to all of the kids and joined us on family occasions whenever she could. We almost always saw her at Thanksgiving and during the Christmas holidays.

Over the next few years, Dell made clear how well her business was doing. From time to time, she mentioned a man named Craig, an architect working with Black & Cooper, the well-known, international construction behemoth that built anything anywhere their clients desired—railroads in India, a new port in Taiwan, oil drilling platforms, skyscrapers, huge shopping malls.

Then one day, three years after we first ran into Dell, we received seven envelopes, edged in gold and addressed in elegant cursive—one for each of us. The cards inside were from the Bondis: "John and Milly Bondi are pleased to announce the marriage of their daughter, Delilah Edna Bondi to Craig Beauchene. The ceremony will take place at Honolulu's Halekulani Hotel on Saturday, October 20 at 3:00. Reception to follow."

In the invitations Ginny and I received, we found a handwritten note from Dell saying that she would be sending us round-trip, first-class tickets to Hawaii and that she'd reserved one of the penthouse apartments at the Four Seasons for our use. "I love all of you so much," she wrote. "I know my nerves will be on edge, and I will need you there to help me through. Please come a couple of days early!"

Dell had stuck a post-it on Jimmy's invitation. "737 long-range BBJ, non-stop. All for you, Jimmy!" This sent Jimmy upstairs to his bedroom, two steps at a time, to find a picture of the jet in one of his aviation books so he could learn its specs in detail.

After a couple of days, it dawned on us that this was a heck of a long journey—over 9,000 miles round trip for a four-day wedding, so we decided to spend a week for ourselves before the actual ceremony. When Ginny talked to the reservation agent at the hotel, attempting to add seven days to our penthouse reservation, the agent told us that the pent house was reserved, charges were covered for four nights, and that it would cost $5,000 per night for us to stay before then. That was not going to happen, so we reserved a much less expensive suite on the lowest floor, with no view of the ocean.

Chapter 41

On the day of our departure, Dell sent a long limousine that comfortably seated all of us and easily held our considerable luggage. The driver took us to All American Aviation at Washington National, where the elegant concierge greeted us like old friends and had his assistants take care of our luggage.

When Jimmy saw the big jet waiting just outside the glass door, he immediately grabbed my hand and started pulling me toward the far exit, yelling, "Dad! Look! There it is! Our plane—it's so much bigger than a GulfStream!"

When the exit door opened, Jimmy rocketed up the stairs of the jet. I followed, and as I turned into the cabin, I stopped, amazed by what I saw. The cabin was wider than the one in a GulfStream. The interior was appointed with leather seats, a couch, and tables that folded into desks. A cabin attendant helped us find our seats and buckle in. She gave each of the kids a lollipop.

Jimmy had expressly asked for a seat next to the wing so he could see the complicated high-lift devices that permitted the plane to cruise at high speeds *and* to land at much safer, low speeds. He watched intently as we headed down the runway. At the end of it, the pilot brought the plane to a halt.

Looking out the window at the wing, Jimmy cupped his fingers as if he were a sports caster holding a microphone calling every play at a game. "On the runway. Brakes locked. High bypass ratio turbo fan engines spooled up to maximum takeoff power."

After a moment, he continued, "Brakes released. Engines at full power, blasting down the runway. Approaching V1," and then, with increased excitement, "V2. We're in the air, climbing like a rocket."

After a long pause, he said, "Leading edge slats being drawn in and flaps brought to cruise position. Wings are clean. We are climbing to 38,000 feet."

We soon heard the pilot's voice over the intercom. He directed our attention to one of the television screens that would track our 4,800-mile flight to Hawaii. Once we leveled off, the cabin attendant, "Katherine," according to her name badge, took luncheon orders off a menu that included hamburgers, hot dogs, filet mignon, chicken cordon bleu, assorted vegetables, and more. All the kids ordered hamburgers or hot dogs, except Jackson, who politely asked, "Could I please have a peanut butter and jelly sandwich on Wonder Bread?" That is exactly what he got, along with a bottle of Sprite.

After nine hours of cruising at 38,000 feet, the pilot began our descent into Honolulu. As he slowed, he gradually moved the slats and flaps down, all to Jimmy's play-by-play description.

CHAPTER
42

Going a week early turned out to be the most wonderful thing our family ever did. To splurge even more, we rented a family cabana for the week, where we could change, get out of the sun, and use the bathroom if we needed one. We never had to leave the beach. The reservation also entitled us to a fancy picnic table with an awning.

Almost at once, the kids discovered that they could have beach service: the delivery of whatever they wanted to drink or eat, of course at exorbitant hotel prices. Somehow, Ginny and I just didn't care. We were in Hawaii for a true, exotic vacation. We followed our childrens' leads in ordering refreshments, but we also had dinner in the hotel's five-star restaurant.

Each day, we did the same thing. The kids played in the sand and water—Jimmy practicing his track skills by sprinting along the ocean's edge, Jackson and Grace digging in the sand, and Sarah slathering herself with lotion, hoping for a tan that her friends in D.C. would envy. Beverly spent her days running out towards the approaching surf and then running back as it splashed around her feet, giggling with excitement again and again. Best of all, at the end of our week, all we had to do was step into the elevator and ride to the high penthouse, where things got even better. Our private butlermade certain that all of our belongings went with us.

Young kids have different values than their parents, so, initially, the younger ones were upset that they were so far from the beach, until we explained that what goes up must come down and all we had to do was take the elevator down. At the end, we stressed that our vacation was over, and it was time for us to get ready to meet Dell and prepare for her wedding.

CHAPTER
43

In the few days before the wedding, Dell, Craig, Ginny, and I made a conscious decision to make time to be together so that Ginny and I could get to know Craig and he could get to know us. As I think back, our first dinner together was the most joyous of the whole affair, apart from the wedding itself.

Craig turned out to be an erudite, Renaissance man—a Quebecois—who spoke Arabic fluently, in addition to his native French and English. He had a diploma from McGill University in Montreal, a master's in architecture from Cornell, and had gone directly to Black & Cooper at a six-figure salary.

Craig had designed buildings all over the world, but he was no stuffed shirt. He had a wonderful, self-deprecating sense of humor and could speak easily on any subject— whether or not it made sense to buy gold or the statistics tracking the performance of his beloved Montreal Canadiens in the National Hockey League.

What also came through loud and clear to both me and Ginny was his sex appeal. He was not handsome in the traditional sense. He had a pock marks on his cheeks and his teeth were slightly crooked. Regardless of his looks, though, there was something about him, a certain *je ne sais quoi* that draws women to men everywhere.

Craig's love for Dell came through loud and clear. He'd been a bit of a rake, but he had finally settled down and made the right choice. He touched Dell gently and held her hand. He often told her that she was a superb professional engineer, stunningly beautiful, and that he was hers for life. Our dinner conversation that night was fluid and filled with laughter. It achieved the goal we all wanted: to get to know each other well. As Ginny and I fell asleep that night, we were both so happy for Dell.

The wedding was stunningly beautiful. Dell's wedding gown was a simple, straight dress that hugged her waist and then fell gracefully to the floor. Craig's tuxedo was elegant—obviously made to measure by a talented tailor. His black shoes gleamed—also obviously custom made—and I caught occasional glimpses of a gold Rolex on his wrist.

When the minister intoned, "You may kiss the bride," Craig bent a little toward Dell, and she stood on her toes. Their lips met and stayed there as the two of them engaged in one of the longest and most intense kisses I have ever seen at a wedding. The guests stood, clapped, and cheered, until finally the minister tactfully cleared his throat. Their lips parted as the cheering continued. They walked down the aisle and out into the gorgeous Hawaiian sun towards the tent where the reception was to take place.

I cannot even guess what the wedding cost, but I know it was a lot more than Ginny's and mine. It was an unmitigated bash!

Chapter 42

Finally, as the guests began to leave, the four of us walked together to the ocean-side park across the street from the hotel. It was dotted with palm trees and orchids and other flowers common to Hawaii. The four of us locked arms as we walked through the park toward the sea.

Suddenly, I felt a sense of love between us all: Dell, Craig, Ginny, and me. I knew with absolute certainty that no matter how far away from each other we might be, and no matter where we were, we would always be together.

ACKNOWLEDGMENTS

Most of all, I must acknowledge the help of my dear wife, Kesaya E. Noda, who brought to bear her substantial, professional skills at editing and writing in the realization of this book. (You get a free copy, dearest!)

CHRISTOPHER DYE

Born in 1944, Christopher Dye grew up in Rochester, New York. After gaining a BA from Haverford College and a JD from Cornell University, he practiced law at the Legal Aid Defender Society in Kansas City, Missouri; Crane & Inker in Boston, Massachusetts; in the law office of Thomas C. Troy in Dorchester, Massachusetts; in private practice in Bradford, Vermont; and at Leahy, Denault, Connair & Hodgman in Claremont, New Hampshire.

Dye remembers:

My time in Kansas City was one of the highlights of my life. As part of a core of VISTA volunteers providing services to indigent clients, we tried numerous cases, some of which were appealed to the Missouri Supreme Court. At the appellate hearing the chief justice thanked us on behalf of the entire court for the high quality of the defense we provided.

Made in the USA
Columbia, SC
10 February 2023

21b0032f-7d4d-4291-8c1b-42ab1b8acb39R02